"When I heard about Ever. enough I wanted to read it. Then I couldn't stop! The band-aid on the front cover is perfect because while everyone says they are fine they're really not. The stories help us know we're not the only ones."

Matthew
Age 17

"*Everything's Fine* is a book I think a lot of kids my age will resonate with. The stories show how tough experiences can be overcome with time and faith in God. It's truly an inspiring book!"

Ashton
Age 16

"The stories of so many vulnerable teens in *Everything's Fine* have made me, a recovering teen, wish I'd had this book a few years ago. Mr. Sikes has provided me with tools to help my small group of soon-to-be freshmen girls to adjust to the new and unknown of high school and to reinforce the message of purposeful hope. I will not hesitate to share this resource with everyone I know who regularly interacts with this precious group.

Emma
Age 23

"The miraculous testimonies described in this book give us a glimpse at the burning heart of God for the next generation. My only response as a sixteen-year-old is to do what Dean has done: say *yes* to the call of God. What the Lord has done through Dean in his ministry has not only massively impacted me, but countless other teenagers."

Maxx
16 Years Old

"Dean Sikes has done a great job of tenderly showing how much my generation is hurting. He equips us with the weapon of the Word to heal, rest, and then arise to be all God says we are!"

Sarah
Age 19

"From the first story you'll find yourself drawn into the lives of real teens facing real problems. What do you do when you're struggling? Are you at the end and ready to simply give up? *Everything's Fine* offers real hope and help that reminds you that if you have breath, you have purpose! Not just stories and questions but relatable insights and answers based on God's truth followed by prayers prayed for you and opportunities to process what you or a friend may be going through."

Sadie Robertson Huff
Author, Speaker, and Founder of Live Original

"The stories and testimonies in the book came alive while I was reading, revealing the silent struggles that today's teens are facing, often alone without much of the support system that I had during my formative years. As you move through the chapters you'll see the hope and redemption that comes as you're introduced to Jesus, the One who loves us and causes each of us to matter. Written for teenagers from all walks of life, *Everything's Fine* can help you come face-to-face with the truth that sets us free. I encourage you to read this book, be encouraged, and find hope when life really hurts."

Michael W. Smith
Award-winning Singer and Musician

"*You matter.* These two words have the potential to shift someone from a place of despair onto a path of destiny. It's a powerful tool to equip parents, teachers, coaches—all who desire to eradicate teen depression and suicide!"

John Bevere
Bestselling Author and Minister
Co-founder of Messenger International & MessengerX

"This message has reached students across our country and world with great effect, restoring children's hope and faith in themselves. As parents, teachers, and administrators search for ways to positively impact their students, I urge them to consider this program to ensure their children hear the life-changing words *you matter.*"

Bill Lee
Governor, State of Tennessee

"Many of you who have picked up this book are trying to figure out life. I can relate. My mother was raped at age forty, and while I'm thankful she gave me life, most of my childhood was turbulent. Because we moved so much, I was never picked for a team. I ate lunch by myself in the cafeteria. Daily, I experienced rejection. But God transformed my life at age fifteen. He showed me that I had value and became the perfect Father I so desperately wanted. God has filled you with potential and has a plan for you too. This book shows you the importance of putting an end to the destruction that can take root when you've been hurt by others. I pray you will read with an open heart and allow God to set you free.

James Robison
Founder and President
LIFE Outreach International
Fort Worth, Texas

EVERYTHING'S
FINE

OTHER BOOKS BY DEAN SIKES

Hope 365

Accepted

The Holy Spirit: Comforter. Counselor. Friend.

EVERYTHING'S
FINE

Finding Hope When Life Really Hurts

DEAN SIKES

You
Matter
Publishing

Published in association with Books, Bach & Beyond, Inc. d/b/a Creative Enterprises Studio, 1507 Shirley Way, Suite A, Bedford, TX 76022. CreativeEnterprisesStudio.com.

While all the stories in this book are true, some names and identifying details have been changed to protect the privacy of the people involved.

Library of Congress Control Number: 2024915198
Softcover: 979-8-9888966-9-2
e-Book: 979-8-9910047-0-1

Cover Design: Kristen Ingebretson
Interior Design: Inside-Out Design & Typesetting, Bedford, TX

Printed in the United States of America

24 25 26 27 28 29 WPP 6 5 4 3 2 1

To every teen and preteen
and those who love and care for them.

Don't suffer alone . . .

If you're struggling and find that
you're having thoughts of harming yourself
help is just three numbers away.

Dial 988

It's a national network of local crisis centers
that provide free and confidential emotional support
to anyone in emotional distress.
Available 24/7/365
in the United States.

CONTENTS

Part Two: *The Path to Hope and Healing*

YOU ARE NOT ALONE

There are 1.3 billion adolescents in the world today, and they make up 16 percent of the world's population. That's a lot of people. If you count yourself among these 1.3 billion, then know this: I wrote this book not just *for* you but *to* you.

Maybe you are beyond the teenage, adolescent years. You are a parent, grandparent, aunt or uncle, high school principal, counselor, youth pastor, or teacher. If so, this book is not written *to* you but as a tool *for* you to use to help understand those you care so much about.

Irrespective of your age, and wherever you find yourself, if life has thrown pain in your direction, don't give up and don't give in. Because despite what you may have encountered or experienced, you are not alone. There is always, *always* help, hope, and healing available to see you through.

Instead, turn the page and let's go on a journey together to discover two words that can forever change your life.

AISLE 21 AT HOME DEPOT

I t began innocently enough. But then it always does. They were friends at school and church. Two guys. One fifteen, the other seventeen. Not best friends but the kind that recognize each other in the hallway with a "Hey, how ya doin'?" nod that communicates something while saying nothing. The younger boy had good grades but a serious issue with being bullied at lunchtime. Every day, dread overwhelmed him as he walked into the cafeteria and looked for the most obscure seat in the all-too-small room. It was a nice try, but it never worked.

One Wednesday afternoon the last bell of the school day rang. Finally, another day was behind him. Eager to get away from the memories of the day and the homework that was in front of him, he agreed to hop into the car of a seventeen-year-old friend from church—an only child who drove a fast sports car. The plan? Go to his house, play some sports, and be back at church in time for the family dinner at 6:00 p.m.

When they arrived at his friend's very large three-story home and said hello to his family, he was invited to his friend's bedroom to see a new electronic gadget he'd been given the previous weekend. When the door was shut, he thought, *Hmm, that's weird,* but the new gadget had his full attention. Invited to sit on the bed, he never saw, never dreamed what would come next. Like a masterful magician whose sly hands moved like the wind, the seventeen-year-old abuser's hands flew all over him. He was stunned, not really grasping what was happening. He wasn't able to think what he could do to stop the horrid insanity, because sixty seconds later it was over. Not missing a beat, the abuser got up, smiled, and asked the boy, "Want to go downstairs and play Ping-Pong?" Not able to speak, the boy nodded his approval as they went downstairs. He played in a state of complete bewilderment. Before long they were back in the sports car, driving to church. They walked in and ate dinner together like nothing had happened.

Except it had.

WHAT'S GOING ON?

This may not be your story. Yours may be much worse! But it is a story experienced by hundreds of thousands of teens each year. The National Children's Alliance reports that 600,000 children and young people under the age of eighteen, at least one in seven,[1] were victims of abuse and neglect in 2021.[2] But that number is considered low due to underreporting because of the COVID-19 pandemic that year. Suffice it to say, there are more than 42 million survivors of sexual abuse in America.[3] Still, somewhere between 66 and 90 percent of victims never tell!

This is why, in June 1989, God asked me to do something for Him. In essence, He said, "Dean, there are generations of teenagers I need you to reach for Me. These kids have no idea that I'm alive, that I love them, and that I have a purpose and a plan for their lives. Many are living with intense pain. I want you to go on the road and give them hope. My hope."

Since January 1993 I've done just that, living out my calling full time, sharing God's truth and His words of hope at more than four thousand events at high schools across America and around the world. To date I've spoken to 2.5 million students in eight countries. Our team has seen more than 150,000 suicides prevented. I've published thirty-two books that serve as follow-up resources. And most importantly to us, at our events we've had more than 300,000 teenagers give their hearts to God!

This book is another act of obedience as I came to realize I can only speak to so many people in person. So, with much prayer and dependence on God, I'll be introducing you to stories of real teens like you who I've met on this journey of faith, students who've courageously shared their personal accounts with me. These are stories that, among others, have shown that it's possible to turn

- pain into purpose,
- anger into passion,

- rejection into acceptance, and

- forgiveness into freedom.

All of the stories point to a unique hope-filled life message and pathway to finding courage, confidence, connection, and answers to the age-old questions of why am I here and what am I supposed to do when things don't turn out like I thought. Written to help eradicate hopelessness and point away from harmful coping practices (including suicide), the end goal is an encounter with the One who, so many decades ago, birthed two words in my heart: **You matter.** These words can absolutely, positively change the trajectory of any person anywhere in the world.

How do I know?

The fifteen-year-old in the story above was me.

WHAT HAPPENED NEXT

After the abuse I went into full denial mode. I figured if I didn't talk about it, maybe it never really happened. But that was a lie. It did happen, along with other things that formed the man I became. Things like abandonment, finding my mom in the middle of her own suicide attempt, and how I, for decades, tried to fill the void in my heart with the things the world said represented power, success, and access to the good life. These possessions, beliefs, and practices turned me into a prideful individual who was simply trying to find acceptance. In all honesty I didn't like myself. I wrongly believed I needed to create an image of myself that others would embrace.

Twenty-two years after that abuse, married and holding the hands of two of my three children, I was walking into Home Depot—something I rarely do because I'm not Mr. Fixer-Upper. When we rounded a corner, I walked right into the person who had sexually abused me when I was fifteen. In that instant I was immediately thrown back into his bedroom. I couldn't speak. My world was unraveling at warp speed. We acknowledged each other, and while I held tightly to my kids' hands, I turned and made a beeline for the nearest exit. I quickly buckled the kids into their car seats and somehow, with my heart racing and my mind reeling, drove safely back home. Sitting there at dinner that night, I knew it was time to deal with the abuse.

WHAT ABOUT YOU?

So what does this have to do with you?

My hope, my goal, my absolute prayer is that, as you read the following stories of real teens in real-life scenarios, you will discover you are not alone in your struggles and there is hope for you to have a better future.

With that, each chapter to come is designed to highlight a trigger that sparks emotional wounds you may have experienced. Those difficult, traumatizing, negative events or set of events and experiences may have caused you mental and psychological pain.[4] And if your wound was caused by someone you knew well as a friend, a teacher, a mentor, or a family member, and it's a deep wound, your pain can go on and on, lasting weeks, months, even years.

But it doesn't have to be that way. Yes, pain hurts, but as long as there is breath in your lungs, there is hope. There is hope that you *will* heal and your life *will* have purpose, meaning, and even joy! I'll share more about this hope throughout the book, but for the moment just know the journey will be worth the effort.

At the end of each chapter you will find practical helps and questions to enable you to process your experiences and emotions. There will be prayers prayed over you and space for you to journal, in your own handwriting, how you're feeling in the moment and to also document where you want to go and how you'll get there.

I am so eager for you to experience God's words and promises found in the Bible! They present truth that's real truth, because it's always true, and they will provide the wisdom and strength you will need to overcome the evil that is always attempting to take over your life. Many verses are sprinkled throughout the book, but they can also be found listed together at the back of the book, along with a few other resources.

It's time to open your mind and your heart. Are you ready?

Let's go!

Dean Sikes is not a licensed therapist. The advice in this book is simply his answer to God's call on his life that was confirmed by the words found in Ezekiel 3:10–11 (NKJV).

Moreover He said to me:
"Son of man, receive into your heart all My words
that I speak to you, and hear with your ears.
And go, get to the captives,
to the children of your people,
and speak to them and tell them,
'Thus says the Lord GOD,'
whether they hear, or whether they refuse."

Part 1

What's **Really** *Going On?*

CHAPTER 1

The Pressure to Perform

It was chilly the morning we arrived at the high school situated in front of a mountain range so beautiful we couldn't help but pause, pull out our phones, and take a few mandatory selfies. But we had to move quickly. We were on a mission. You could even call it a mission from God, because quite literally He *was* the reason we were there.

After the team snapped some photos, we gathered our things, and the three of us walked to the main doors of the building.

Clearing a metal detector, we moved to the office, where we met the principal. After hellos and handshakes, we were escorted to the auditorium where, in a few minutes, the all-school assembly was scheduled. Students were already filing in through four different entrances. As the thousand-plus teens looked for a seat to occupy for the next forty minutes, I noticed three groups of people.

Group one walked in as if they owned the place. Outwardly confident, their very presence commanded attention. Group two quietly walked past their fellow classmates.

They identified their seats and quickly sat down, hoping to blend in and not stand out. Then there was group three, always my favorite. They were the guys coolly watching the girls as they walked in, inwardly questioning if they knew they were being watched. (If by chance you find yourself in group three, the answer is yes, they know you're watching!)

After calling the students to order and making a brief introduction, the principal handed me the microphone. As I've done more than four thousand times, I began a conversation with the teens seated in front of me. No notes, no canned speech. Just an invitation to invest some time with one another, to connect, and to go on a journey together—a journey based on stories from the road I've been traveling for thirty-plus years.

The stories are as varied as the people in the room. These included anecdotes from bullying to abandonment, from body image issues to cutting, as well as the stress of expectations by not just teachers and parents but the world that surrounds us, both real and online. Yet they all have one common theme: an emotional wound that results in feelings of helplessness and hopelessness.

THREE QUESTIONS

Walking up and down the aisles of the auditorium this autumn morning I found the more stories I shared, the more emotional issues that were introduced, the more the students were drawn in. Everyone loves stories. Maybe it's the relatability factor or the way stories grab our heart without warning. Simply put, stories help us to see ourselves. This day was no exception.

During the assembly there were times of full-blown laughter. At other times the silence was deafening. Somewhere in between the story and the takeaway (namely, exposure to and acknowledgement of the realities of life), the gathered students met their own personal vulnerabilities. The arrow hits its intended mark—the heart.

Vulnerability, the inability to resist something hazardous or disastrous, evokes different emotions. To one it might be tears. To another there is a conscious choice to push down the emotions attempting to take them hostage and temporarily escape from reality. Others give a dismissive eye roll that says *I'm bored and, by the way, who do you think you are? And what do you know anyway?*

Thirty minutes passed way too fast. As the assembly drew to a close, I searched every section of the auditorium, looking for what would come next. My heart began to literally pound inside my chest. I know this feeling all too well—it's when God's Spirit begins to move and I recognize it's time to throw the net. It's time to ask three questions that, when answered, bring the listeners face-to-face with the unfailing power of love. What happens next is always as personal as the people who respond.

I ask everyone in the auditorium to close their eyes and draw an imaginary circle around their life. I tell them I'm about to ask them three very important questions and that it's essential they focus on each one, answering as honestly as they can. Then, in the peaceful quietness, I share how I have this pounding inside of me, in the center of my chest. I invite them to acknowledge that many of them, too, are experiencing the same internal feeling. Except the pounding is not an emotional feeling, it's a Person. It's Jesus making Himself known. Why? Because He wants to lead them out of their pain, to help them know that their life matters and that God has a plan and a purpose for their lives.

Pausing after each question, I invite the students to respond by raising their hand if their answer is yes. Right now, in this auditorium, for these one thousand students, it's decision time. What will they decide? What will they choose?

Question 1: Is there someone in your life who's really hurt you? After hearing the stories today, do you believe the right decision is for you to forgive this person? If your answer is yes, raise your hand.

Response: more than 735 hands shoot into the air.

Question 2: If you, like me, know the pain of being rejected and abandoned, but you want to know the kindness and feeling of absolute joy of being accepted, would you raise your hand?

Response: more than 470 hands go up.

Question 3: If you feel like you don't matter, if you think no one would miss you if you weren't here, if you've bought the lie that your death is a better choice than living your life, if suicide is a real option for you, please raise your hand. *Response:* 53 brave students courageously raise their hands, indicating that suicide is on their minds!

My heart is filled with empathy as I watch each hand go up. I want to sit with them, listen to them, assure them that, despite how dark life might seem or be for them, it's always darkest when you don't have any light. Jesus, the Light of the World, is simply waiting for them to ask Him to eradicate their darkness!

I quickly run my hands across my eyes to wipe away the tears as I see so many hurting students. Then, to seize the moment, my heart reminds me to lead them into an opportunity to get help, to introduce them to our follow-up resources that live online at our website, www.youmatter. us. There they will find resources that are free anywhere 24/7/365, if they can access the internet.

AN UNEXPECTED RESPONSE

I closed the assembly that day by inviting the principal back to the stage. As he walked up, I thanked the students for allowing me to have this time with them and then told them I was available to chat with them if any of them wanted to stay for a few minutes.

No matter the venue—public, private, Christian, Catholic, alternative, juvenile detention center, teen challenge center—every school has students who want to talk after-ward. This day was no different. Many students stayed to talk. What *was* different, however, was the young man I watched walk down the aisle with eight of what I gathered were his friends following him. Leadership dripped off this kid and these eight guys were pursuing it.

We shook hands and the leader turned to his friends and asked them to give us a few minutes. He'd meet them at lunchtime. The eight young men turned and dutifully exited the auditorium, likely heading for the cafeteria. I was standing in the now empty and quiet auditorium with a young man I'll call Grant. Moments earlier the room had been bustling with students. Now they were all either head-ing to lunch or to their next class.

Grant began by sharing how much he appreciated the assembly. I thanked him and invited him into a conversa-tion that was intended to give me some insight into who he was. He said he was a junior, had a 3.8 GPA, was the quarterback of the varsity football team (which immediately gave insight into his leadership capacity), had a supportive family, and was dating a very special girl. Without pausing, he added, "Oh, yeah, and this Friday night we're playing in the state championship football game—and we're going to win."

As I took in all that he was sharing, I reiterated each point back to him and said, "Sure seems like you're living a dream life." Suddenly the smile left his face, tears filled his eyes, and it was clear that life for Grant was not a dream. At least, not the dream one would *want* to experience.

Grant looked into my eyes and bravely said, "I raised my hand for all three of your questions." I was dumbfounded. Here was an obviously very popular young man with everything appearing to be going his way. Yet he struggled with the need to feel accepted as he was, he was overwhelmed by the pressure of expectations regarding his performance, and he needed to forgive those who had either knowingly or unknowingly placed them on him. But most alarmingly, he wanted to die. Suddenly it was all too clear. Everything was *not* fine.

Grant could see my perplexed look. Before giving me an opportunity to ask my probing questions to better understand what had brought him to this point in his life, the quarterback took the lead. His next sentence gave light to what he was experiencing. With tears streaming down his face, he said, "Mr. Dean, you cannot imagine the pressure to perform that I live with every hour of every day. It's too much and I can't take it anymore." He reached into his pocket and pulled out a shotgun shell. He handed it to me and said, "This afternoon at 3:15 I was going to the football field, not to practice, but to end my life. Today you told me that my life matters and that God has a plan for me. I choose to believe you, so will you please take this shell?"

I tried to gather my thoughts, but honestly all I knew to do was to put my arms around him, this guy who seemingly had it all, and give him a hug. Our embrace wasn't long, but it was meaningful. I asked Grant if he'd be open to some truth that could change his life right then and there. He immediately agreed, so I quoted a verse from the bestselling book of all time, the Bible, where it says, "The Spirit of God has made me, and the breath of the Almighty gives me life" (Job 33:4 NKJV). I asked Grant, "Who made you?" He replied, "The Spirit of God." Then I said, "Whose breath gave you life?" He answered, "The Almighty."

Grant was beginning to see that what was being shared was for him and his life. God's truth about who he was and to whom his allegiance belonged began to anchor in his soul. The tears that only seconds ago were welling up and freely flowing gave way to a smile that began in his heart and quickly shot across his face. Why? Because truth, God's truth, will always set us free (John 8:32)!

I gave Grant a second big hug and connected him with the school counselor for some additional help. As he walked away from our meeting, I watched him go and my heart was so full of gratitude for what the Lord had just done.

WHAT ABOUT YOU?

How does Grant's story relate to you? You may not be a quarterback, have a GPA you care for anyone to know, or any of the other things Grant mentioned, but the absolute truth is that you, too, were created on purpose, with purpose, and for a purpose. God has never, ever made a mistake, and He certainly didn't make one when He made you and put His breath in you to give you life. It's why I can say with absolute certainty and confidence the same two words I said to Grant that day, the two words that can change your life forever when life hurts and you need hope and healing.

You matter!

You are why I wrote this book! I realized I can only physically go to a limited number of schools for this kind of assembly. But you (yes, you!) are absolutely on my radar. Consider this as me looking straight into your eyes and asking you to consider the same three questions I asked Grant.

1. Has someone really hurt you?
2. Do you know the pain of being rejected and abandoned?
3. Do you feel like you don't matter?

It's not unusual for athletes and those who function in a public space to experience the pressure to perform. But this kind of pressure is inescapable in all our lives—that is, if you live in a setting that involves other people. We all have expectations of ourselves and of each other. Some personalities can blow off what another person might want or expect of them. Others, not so much, because they care too much about what someone else thinks.

What about you? What pressures do you feel? Do those pressures affect you in a way that causes you to question yourself?

TRUTH FROM THE CHAPTER

Let's recap a few of the truths from this chapter to internalize and remember.

- God made you to be unique, which means you don't have to be like anyone else.
- If you've achieved some level of notoriety, remember it's inhuman to expect to stay at that level. Life is full of ebb and flow, ups and downs. It's okay and it's supposed to be that way!
- Expectations are not often based on reality; only accurate expectations are useful for making good choices. Work toward properly identifying which expectations are helpful.
- You'll never be able to please everyone, so create a mental list of who is important enough to cause you to plan your life according to their thoughts and needs. (It needs to be a short list.)
- Learn to live for an audience of one: God.

TRUTH FROM GOD'S WORD

Come to me, all of you who are tired and have heavy loads, and I will give you rest. Accept my teachings and learn from me, because I am gentle and humble in spirit, and you will find rest for your lives. The burden that I ask you to accept is easy; the load I give you to carry is light.
(Matt. 11:28–30)

In all the work you are doing, work the best you can.
Work as if you were doing it for the Lord, not for people.
Remember that you will receive your reward from the
Lord, which he promised to his people. You are serving
the Lord Christ.

(Col. 3:23–24)

MY PRAYER FOR YOU

Thank you, Father, for the power of Your truth that
reminds these kids that You made them and gave them
breath; which means our allegiance is to You, not anyone
else who might choose to put their expectations on us.
Including ourselves! It's all about You and for You. Amen.

In the following space or in a separate journal write the
answers to these questions. Since this is your story, be
honest with yourself. It's the only way to truly change your
life forever!

Have you felt the pressure to perform? If so, recap the
instance(s) here.

_____

_____

_____

_____

_____

How can you change your thought processes to keep this from ruling your life?

_____

_____

_____

_____

CHAPTER 2

So Lonely I Could Die

Walking into a school for one of our assemblies always begins with deep feelings of compassion and a high level of expectancy for what is about to happen. Today was no different, except that something felt off when we met the school receptionist. Maybe we were tired from the early morning wake-up call. More likely it was because of the perplexed look on the woman's face when we explained we were there for the afternoon assembly scheduled to begin in fifteen minutes. Asking again for our names, she made a phone call. It was when we overheard her asking someone if they knew anything about an event that we realized our high level of expectancy this time was ours alone. The assembly had not made it onto the school calendar.

We waited for twenty minutes to see what was going to happen. Gratefully, we received confirmation that the students would soon be gathering in the gymnasium.

It had already been a busy day, and before it ended we had been in two states at five separate events and spoken to more than sixteen hundred students. On days like these, our logistics are planned out to the minute. And every minute has to be prescheduled by our team. Any deviation immediately puts what came next at the risk of not being possible.

Joseph, one of our ministry team members, and I were pacing up and down the hall. Because we had one more event after this one, I was tempted to rush through our presentation to make up the lost time. It's a full-on internal struggle in my mind.

With my thoughts bouncing from side to side, like a pinball launched into full-on game mode, I sorted through the stories I should tell, struggling with what was best for me to share. As my frustration increased, my pacing intensified.

And then Joseph very quietly said, "This is going to be a powerful assembly. Lives are going to be forever changed."

Peace immediately permeated my heart. As it did, God's message for this specific group of teens began to form in my mind. I looked up and saw the steady stream of people filling the gym. After a very brief introduction, we began our program.

ALONE ON THE BACK ROW

From the students' response, it was obvious what God had wanted communicated was resonating. When our time together came to an end, the students exited the gym, but as they were leaving, I slowed down my thoughts about needing to move on to the next school and surveyed the room to see if anyone had stayed behind. This was most often the best way to find someone who wants an opportunity to talk to me but is afraid to ask.

As I scanned the room, I noticed a young man, let's call him Sean, who had remained seated all alone on the back row. Despite the chaotic activity around him, Sean had kept his focus on me. When our eyes connected, I walked toward him.

After a hello, with a quiet tone to his voice, he shared how much our message had affected him. Ignoring the time, I thanked him and sat down next to him—offering an unspoken invitation to share with me whatever was erupting in his heart. What was clear was that Sean's emotions had been stirred during our assembly.

THE DEAL WITH EMOTIONS

What are emotions? They are our feelings, our reactions, often triggered by what happens to us in life. Created by God, they help us process our experiences. One of the most important lessons I've learned after decades of speaking is that if you don't deal with your emotions, your emotions will surely deal with you—often in an unkind way. How we process, exhibit, and deal with them is important and is as unique as each person.

The initial emotion Sean displayed was anger, but as he talked, his anger turned to sadness. He began to open a painful wound he'd buried deep inside. The sadness in his eyes told even more of a story than perhaps his heart wanted to willingly relive. But as he talked, it became clear that this conversation was the reason we were at this school.

As he struggled to find the right words, I encouraged Sean to not worry about how it sounded but to simply share whatever came to him and affirmed that I'd be listening.

Listening has become a lost art. It's not even that we necessarily want to talk, but everyone desperately desires to be heard. This is important, because if we do not feel heard, then we begin to believe our voice, and therefore our life, does not matter. And when we don't feel as if we matter, hopelessness crashes over and into our emotions and even our actions.

This fact was confirmed in a recent survey conducted by the Centers for Disease Control (CDC).[1] The survey clearly identified the often-overlooked factor among teen-agers who are suffering emotionally is that they do not feel seen or heard. This same survey reported "44% of high school students reported experiencing persistent feelings of sadness or hopelessness in the past year." These two statistics—not feeling seen or heard and experiencing feel-ings of sadness or hopelessness—are unquestionably and undeniably connected. Every week my team sees this emo-tional connection playing out in the lives of students from quite literally every walk of life.

Before he responded to me, Sean took a deep breath, awkwardly swayed in his seat, and tested the waters to see how much he could share. I'm not sure he was on a search for answers as much as he was on a quest to be heard and maybe even to be validated in what he was feeling. The more he talked, the more I settled into my seat and just listened. In moments such as this, time is not important.

Sean said, "I waited for you because I felt like I needed to let you know what I'm going through, and for some reason, I immediately trusted you with things I have never told anyone in my life." He shared how he was an angry little boy who, as he was growing up, often fought with his brother and sister. His mother reached out to professionals in the medical community to determine "how best to deal with someone like me." It was decided she would put a lock on his bedroom door and latch the lock in the hallway, preventing him from coming and going as he pleased. Sean had to wait for his mother to let him out of his room whether it was for meals, a bathroom break, or to go somewhere. He was literally serving a sentence of isolation.

Sean went on to describe the loneliness he felt and how much he hated being separated from his siblings. He had also been banned from having any electronics in his room. He truly felt alone, unseen, and unheard. Sitting there in isolation soon gave way to creativity. He devised a plan to unlock the door from the inside. While it freed him from his one-room house arrest, his newfound freedom was short lived. He quickly returned to fighting with his family members, which landed him in an intensive therapy program. As Sean described it, for him, the therapy sessions were less than helpful. One day he had had enough. Bolting out of a therapist's office, he ran, searching for a place to cry.

Pausing for a moment, Sean looked intently into my eyes, no doubt to ensure I was still listening and that he was indeed being heard. Taking a deep breath, he resumed his story.

At the breaking point, and in desperation for both Sean and his parents, he was institutionalized. During his stay at the hospital a diagnosis was made, medication was prescribed, and the anger with which he had lived for so long began to diminish. What did not diminish, however, was his inability to trust anyone. He told me that he stopped talking to others, only responded when asked direct questions, and then reiterated once again that he trusted no one.

Clearly, everything was *not* fine.

One day, wrestling with thoughts of suicide, along with the lie that there was no hope in sight, that ending it all was his only way out of a life of isolation, anger, and sadness, he said, "Something told me not to." With that admission, the emotions that were buried deep within Sean's heart began to erupt like a volcano. Tears freely flowed down his face. He had buried the pain for such a long, long time.

THE TRASH CAN

If you have a trash can in your room and you never empty it, but instead keep pushing the trash down deeper and deeper, one day the trash will overflow. It's no different with you and me and our hearts. If we keep pushing down our emotions and trying to live life with a heart full of pain or anger or sadness that we just pile on top, if none of that is dealt with, a day will come when there will be an eruption, an overflow of all of our ignored emotions. And once that overflow begins, it is too difficult to manage. The pain will surface, the tears will flow, and then we will have to deal with it.

Which is exactly what happened. Sean told me that the day he said, "Something told me not to," was the day he had turned to God. Because he had no friends and trusted no one, he had nowhere to turn *but* to God. As those words left his mouth, his heart gave way and the dam of tears broke completely.

I thanked Sean for allowing me to be a listening ear so he could know he'd been heard. He apologized for crying and shared that he'd never told anyone what he'd just told me. He said that, as he had been talking, the pain he'd carried and buried in his heart had started to bust loose and was making its way out. It was obvious he needed to work through his anger and trust issues and to find the power that comes from forgiving those who had hurt him. But for now, being heard had brought him hope.

Being heard brought hope. When I heard him say that, I was immediately reminded of what Joseph had said to me earlier: "This is going to be a powerful assembly. Lives are going to be forever changed." He was right! And I was so very grateful to the Lord for using him to remind me of the importance of living in the moment instead of being focused on and consumed with what's next.

As my team left the school and moved to our final event of the day, our hearts were once again full of expectancy, knowing that, in a few minutes, we'd again have the honor of offering hope to students. I'm not sure how God did it, but somehow we were on schedule!

WHAT ABOUT YOU?

Though you may not have been locked in your bedroom, you may have felt locked up with your inability to be seen and heard. Maybe you've felt isolated from the people around you at school, even at home. You feel invisible.

Just as in Sean's case, there is hope. Just as surely as God was available to Sean, He's available to you right here, right now.

There's a verse in the Bible that comes to my mind. It says, "Call to me and I will answer you" (Jer. 33:3a NIV). If we reach out to God, He will not only hear us, *He will also answer us!* You need never feel invisible or alone again.

TRUTH FROM THE CHAPTER

Let's recap a few of the truths from this chapter to internalize and remember.

- God always has a plan! You might think you're too

late or even too early, but the truth is, if you follow God's leading, you'll always be right on time.

- Emotions are our feelings and reactions that are often triggered by what happens to us and helps us to process our experiences. If you don't deal with your emotions, your emotions will deal with you. So how you process, exhibit, and deal with them is important.

- Like with a trash can, if we keep pushing down our emotions, a day will come when there will be an eruption, an overflow, of all that has been ignored. And once that overflow begins, it is too difficult to manage and you *will* have to deal with it.

- Be a listener because everyone desperately desires to be heard, and being heard brings hope.

- God is always available. You need never feel alone again.

TRUTH FROM GOD'S WORD

Be strong and brave. Don't be afraid of them and don't be frightened, because the LORD your God will go with you. He will not leave you or forget you.

(Deut. 31:6)

"Never will I leave you; never will I forsake you."

(Heb. 13:5 NIV)

MY PRAYER FOR YOU

Today, Jesus, I pray for those who know what it's like to feel invisible or that their life does not matter. I pray for everyone who, like Sean, lives with deep-rooted pain and disappointment from being alone, lonely, and depressed. Meet them where they are. Fill them with Your perfect love that always cares and protects and never gives up. And thank You for Your presence and the assurance that You never leave us or forget us. You are always there waiting, listening for us to call out to You. Hear our prayers, and thank You in advance for the answers that will come. In Your name I pray. Amen.

In the space that follows, or in a separate journal, write the answers to these questions. Since this is your story, be honest with yourself. It's the only way to truly change your life forever!

Are there any issues that you've been putting off acknowledging and dealing with?

_____

_____

_____

_____

_____

What about emotions? Are you pushing something down into your emotional trash can?

_____

_____

_____

_____

_____

Even if you feel alone, God has promised to always be with you. If you could see Him sitting with you right now, what would you say to Him?

_____

_____

_____

_____

_____

_____

_____

_____

_____

CHAPTER 3

I Don't Like What I See

Describe yourself. There are a lot of adjectives available: short, tall, fat, skinny, lean, muscular, flabby, athletic, beautiful, cute, ugly, feminine, masculine, confused. The list could go on and on. But so also do our deepest feelings about ourselves.

As of December 2023, a recent summary of stats and studies[1] tells us:

- More than 40% of boys in middle school and high school regularly exercise with the aim of increasing muscle mass
- About 70% of girls from 15 to 17 years of age avoid normal daily activities such as attending school when they feel bad about their looks
- On average, teenagers see between 600–625 commercials per day—many of which focus on the body and appearance
- Nearly 30% of adolescent girls with poor body satisfaction will go on to develop depression in adulthood

- Among high school students, 44% of girls and 15% of boys are attempting to lose weight
- More than 45% of teenagers feel pressure to have ideal physical appearances from social media
- Only 4% of women globally consider themselves beautiful, many of the concerns about looks start in the teenage years
- Teens who report high levels of exposure to media— such as music videos—have higher levels of body dissatisfaction

The data reveals that body image perceptions are taking a toll on our mental and physical health. And that doesn't begin to touch the surface of more recent issues regarding gender confusion and how that adds to our feelings of being discontent with who we are. No doubt we need a healthier perspective of ourselves.

I'VE NEVER TOLD ANYONE BEFORE

A few years ago a couple who heard me speak at a convention invited us to share our message with the schools in their city. They set up some opportunities for us to speak in their hometown and the surrounding area. We arrived at one of the schools, after back-to-back assemblies at four different schools the previous day, and met the principal and school counselor. They escorted us into a large assembly hall. As is my habit, I stood off alone for a moment and watched as hundreds of teenagers entered the room from various doors. Per usual, the three people groups we identified in chapter 1 were present and most definitely accounted for. You might remember them as the confident leaders, the don't-notice-me majority, and the guys I'll call "the watchers." The assembly concluded after our presentation and a short time of questions and answers, and the teens were dismissed to their next class. On this day, however, not everyone left so quickly. Many stayed back to talk. The principal, recognizing the number of students who stayed in the assembly hall, gave me a green light to talk to them and excused in advance their tardiness when they eventually went to their classes.

These one-on-one conversations with teenagers are my favorite part of being on the road and speaking to students. It's always an honor to be trusted with what is going on in their hearts and lives—at least the part of their story they want to tell us.

With a teacher close by to ensure proper accountability is preserved, each student in the long line that formed waits to tell me his or her story. That's when I met Julie. She walked up with an obvious joy and confidence, not in an offensive way, but covered by an unmistakable humility, and she began talking about the love she has for God. But it's this love, she explains, that makes it difficult to tell me what's really going on. She then asks if I'm familiar with 1 Corinthians 6:19–20, which she quotes from memory: "You should know that your body is a temple for the Holy Spirit who is in you. You have received the Holy Spirit from

God. So you do not belong to yourselves, because you were bought by God for a price. So honor God with your bodies."

As a Christian, Julie knows she has given herself, which includes her body, to God. It is now His temple and the place where His Spirit lives. Which means that what she does with it and to it matters.

I ask Julie to share with me a little about her life at school, home, and whatever she wanted to share. And she does. She's a straight-A student, captain of the cheerleading squad, dating a football player, great home life, and loves her church, where she's very involved in her youth group. As she talks, the genuine smile on her face is impossible to miss. But what is equally impossible to miss is the sadness in her eyes. I thought about Matthew 6:22, which tells us our eyes are the lamp or the light of our body. If our eyes are good, our whole body will be full of light.

Sitting on the edge of the stage, listening to the captain of the cheerleading squad tell me how great her life is, I couldn't help but wonder why her eyes looked so terribly dark and sad.

I ask her, "What's really going on? What are you wanting to talk about but afraid to mention?"

Hearing those questions unlock the emotional dam and release a wave of tears. She tries to regain her composure, but whatever she was trying to hide was now being exposed by the light of truth—the thing that always sets us free.

After wiping the tears from her face, Julie asks how I know there's more for her to share. My response is immediate: "When you walked up to the stage just now, I could see it in your eyes. There is healing available for you today, Julie, but for that to happen you will have to be totally honest with yourself."

I then explain to her I'm simply a listening ear, someone who genuinely cares about her, but the look on her face needs no interpretation as I know she's thinking, *You don't even know me; how can you care about me?*

Before she can ask the question her face is communicating, I say, "I care about you because you're breathing, and you're breathing because God gave you life, and He's never made a mistake."

Julie takes a deep breath and with a newfound confidence says to me, "Mr. Dean, I have an eating disorder and you're the only person I've ever told."

Hearing her words makes my heart ache for her! I want her to know that she's not a bad person, that eating disorders are brutal and are based on lies. I also want her to understand how much God loves her and that she's not alone.

One statistic cited in a CNN report on February 20, 2023,[2] proves it. Researchers reviewed and analyzed thirty-two studies from sixteen countries and found that 22 percent of children and adolescents showed disordered eating behaviors. It seems body image is a struggle around the world!

Julie tells me how much shame she lives with every single day. 24/7/365. She knows what she is doing to her body, the temple of the Holy Spirit, is wrong, which brings with it so much guilt. The more she talks, the more I listen. Then she tells me something I already know. For a significantly large percentage of young women who today are suffering with an eating disorder, the disorder has not so much to do with weight but much more to do with control.

We'll talk more about this control issue in the next chapter, but for now it's important to recognize something. We live in a world that constantly feels like it's about to spin out of control—especially our control—so we often subconsciously work extra hard to offset it by attempting to control something or someone else we *can* control.

Julie and I talk a bit more, but soon it's time for her to go to class and for me to go to the next school. Before saying goodbye, I ask if she would allow me to accompany her to the school counselor's office so a trained professional can walk her through her eating disorder and on to emotional health. At first Julie resists, but then something changes. She looks at me, but this time her eyes are no longer dark and sad. They are full of light! She says, "Mr. Dean, I think God just spoke to me, telling me to go get help. And if I do, my life will be forever changed. Will you go with me to the counselor's office?"

We walk directly to the counselor's office. With Julie's permission, I share with the counselor what she had shared with me. I then excuse myself and leave Julie in a safe place with someone who will help her navigate a journey of healing, a journey that will take her from shame and pain to forgiveness, healing, and hope.

IT'S NOT JUST ABOUT EATING

Since the day I met Julie at her high school and she courageously opened up and shared some of her story with me, I've communicated parts of her testimony to thousands of teens, many of whom could immediately relate to the trappings and pain associated with eating disorders. In recent years I've had several young men take the same steps of faith, letting me know that they, too, are dealing with an eating disorder. It seems to have risen to an all-time high during the years of our ministry.

But it's not just about the image that's affected by our eating habits and overall health routines in our attempt to look a certain way. There's also the image we edit, the way we portray ourselves online, which we will cover in chapter 7. It's a constant comparison that becomes a great source of suffering and leads to major discontent and depression.

Then there's the not-really-new issue that's growing in awareness and acceptance: discontent with the gender God created you to be. Here's some truth to consider. God knows you better than you know yourself. And He's known you much longer than you've inhabited Planet Earth. How do we know? Check out Jeremiah 1:5 (NIV): "Before I formed you in the womb I knew you, before you were born I set you apart; I appointed you as a prophet to the nations." God not only created the world, He created you! In His infinite wisdom, God created you to be the person you were born to be!

Why is this important to understand?

Though we may be confused about who we are, God is not. He always has a plan, which means He always knows exactly what He is doing. And here's the most important thing for you to know: Whether you know the true you, whether you choose to embrace who you were created to be, God absolutely loves you! Not an inconsistent, unreliable, limited love, but one that cannot be fully understood or in any way earned or contained. There's nothing we could ever do to cause Him to love us more than He already does. The opposite is also true. There is nothing we will ever do to cause Him to love us less than He does.

Simply put, God is love.

Here's another truth. When God created you, He did so on purpose. Not by accident. He also had a purpose, a reason for there to be a you, and then He filled you with His purpose, which is to share His love with others. And if that's not enough, He created you in His likeness to be like Him. This means you are a spirit. You have a soul—your mental battleground that houses your mind, your will, and your emotions. And you live in a body.

Most of the battles you and I will ever fight are in our minds. For instance, if you are confused about who you are and the life God created you to live, the truth is that the confusion did not come from God. First Corinthians 14:33 explains it this way: "God is not a God of confusion but a God of peace. As is true in all the churches of God's people." Did you catch that? God is not a God of confusion. He is a God of peace. If you're confused today, that confusion did not come from God; it came from a real enemy, the devil.

CONFUSED AND STRUGGLING

In recent months our team has come face-to-face with teens who are wrestling with what gender they are and how they will live their lives. This is Tyler's story.

I had just finished speaking at a large public high school and many students walked to the front to say hello and talk to me. As I finished listening to and sharing some thoughts with the last student in line, my team member Joseph pulled me aside and told me there was one more student I really needed to talk with. The look in Joseph's eyes told me it was serious and this conversation needed to happen before we left the school.

I followed him across the gym floor, where I meet Tyler. Leaning against the wall, his eyes were already filling with tears. I introduced myself, we shook hands, and Tyler began by telling me how much he enjoyed our presentation. I thanked him and matter-of-factly asked, "What's going on?"

Maybe it was the directness of my question or perhaps he was just ready to talk. Whatever the reason, Tyler's response was immediate. He looked at me, took a deep breath, and said, "I'm trans. Do I still matter to God?"

As Tyler's words hit my heart, I quickly breathed a prayer, asking God to help me know what to say, to give me words that would meet Tyler where he was. Immediately a response filled my mind. I said, "Tyler, you and I can agree to disagree on your choices and the lifestyle you're currently living, but because you are breathing, yes, without any hesitation of contradiction, God loves you and you matter to Him!"

Hearing those words did something to Tyler's heart, because when he heard that he was loved and that his life does matter to God, he broke down. He cried hard! When he was finally able to speak again, he said the decision to live the life he was living was a direct result of years of being bullied. With tears streaming down both sides of his face he said, "I just could not take the pain anymore. Something had to change."

Tyler and I talked some more, and then, in a moment I hope I never forget, he asked to borrow my pen. I handed it to him. He pulled out our "I Matter" pledge card and said, "Before we talked, I was not going to sign your pledge. But hearing that God still loves me and that I matter to Him, I'm now ready to sign it, choosing life over death." What a thrill, honor, and privilege to be with Tyler as he recognized his value as one of God's own creations!

On our way out of the school I stopped by the principal's office to share with her what had just happened in the gym with Tyler. As I was leaving, the two of them were deep in conversation.

WHAT YOU SEE VERSUS WHAT YOU CAN KNOW

No doubt everything's not fine when we struggle with how we see ourselves. But here's the truth. Your mind is a powerful force! That's why God tells us in Romans 12:2: "Do not be shaped by this world; instead be changed within by a new way of thinking. Then you will be able to decide what God wants for you; you will know what is good and pleasing to him and what is perfect."

You can literally transform your life by making your mind new with truth in the place of the lies the Enemy whispers. Lies such as you're fat, you're ugly, no one likes you, you're a big pain and a fraud, you're not even who or what you think you are.

Instead, I want to speak these truths over your life because no way should you allow the world to tell you who you are. Hear what God, your Creator, your heavenly Father, has to say.

- You are made special and unique by a loving Creator. (Ps. 139:14)
- God has a beautiful plan for your life. (Eph. 2:10)
- God is trustworthy. His Word is true and He does what is right. (Ps. 33:4)

- God won't leave you to do life on your own! (Deut. 31:8)
- God has prepared a place for us with Him in heaven for all eternity! (John 14:3)

Though the data may reveal our body image perceptions are taking a toll on our mental and physical health, we know it does *not* have to be that way. It's time to open our eyes to the truth and see things as they really and truly are.

WHAT ABOUT YOU?

Do you have a hidden secret you are fearful someone's going to find out? Do you live with an uneasiness in your heart that today might be the day the real you is discovered?

Maybe you're wrestling with your identity. You struggle with liking, much less loving yourself. It's easy to listen to and believe the lies in your head, but they are not the truth! Real truth, God's truth as found in the Bible, sets us free.

It's important to know you are not alone! Teenagers around the world are waking up today and experiencing the exact same issues you are facing. Again, you are why I wrote this book, so you'll know you are not the only one. As you continue to read, I pray you find that is true and that there is help and hope for you too!

TRUTH FROM THE CHAPTER

Let's recap a few of the truths from this chapter to internalize and remember.

- For much longer than you have been alive, God has known you and known everything about you. Past, present, and future. And no matter what, He loves you.
- Your relationship with God will never be what it can be if you think you're in a performance-based relationship with Him. He loves you because you are His child, not because of anything you do or don't do.
- Refuse to be defined by society's perceptions and labels. Instead, realize your worth as you discover God's incredible love for you. This discovery begins by reading His Word, the Bible.

TRUTH FROM GOD'S WORD

I praise you because you made me in an amazing and
wonderful way. What you have done is wonderful.
I know this very well.
(Ps. 139:14)

But God shows his great love for us in this way:
Christ died for us while we were still sinners.
(Rom. 5:8)

MY PRAYER FOR YOU

Dear Father in heaven, today I pray for everyone who is reading this book who might be struggling with some type of discontent with themselves. Maybe it's an eating disorder, body image issues, or wondering who they are. I pray the truth of Your Word will permeate their hearts and minds in a way that the truth they know sets them free. I ask in faith that You meet each one of them where they are and through a relationship with Your Spirit, help them see the path You have chosen for them to live. In Jesus' most holy name. Amen.

⁓

In the space that follows, or in a separate journal, write the answers to these questions. Since this is your story be honest with yourself. It's the only way to truly change your life forever!

Can you identify and name three things about yourself that you really like?

_____

_____

_____

_____

_____

_____

If it is important to you to be liked and accepted by others, identify the reasons why.

CHAPTER 4

Razor Blades, Cigarette Lighters, and Other Things That Hurt

It seemed the entire reason we were in Texas was perhaps for this one conversation to occur. After speaking to a gathering of students at the city's convention center and inviting anyone who wanted to talk afterward to join us at our resource table, we began to pack up the items that were left as we prepared to leave. For the third time I looked down to the end of the table to see a young woman who had been standing off to the side, waiting. But she was no longer just standing. She had begun to move toward us.

Megan approached me, extended her hand, and introduced herself. I smiled and said, "My wife and I have a daughter named Megan. We call her Meggie."

She smiled. "That's great, my name is Megan."

I smiled back at her. "Okay, Megan it is."

As she took a deep breath, she said she had enjoyed what I had shared and then matter-of-factly asked, "Can I tell you my story?" I immediately said yes, leaned back against the table, and told her I was ready.

As Megan began to talk, tears formed in her eyes, threatening to make their way down her face. She was now having trouble putting her sentences together. I encouraged her to take a minute, gather her thoughts, and to not rush. We had plenty of time. I thought it might be helpful to get her to open up and talk about herself a little, so I asked her age.

She said, "I'm fourteen years old."

Instantly I wondered what would be so horrific in the life of this young woman that would cause her to have such anxiety and an overwhelming desire to tell a stranger what had brought her to this point in life.

After she regained her composure, Megan talked and I simply listened.

She told me some of her background and experiences and that she didn't feel like she measured up in any way. Then she asked me, "Mr. Dean, can I show you something on my wrist?"

"Sure," I said. And while my response was quick, my reaction to what she showed me was immediate.

Megan pulled her sleeve back, turned her wrist over, and revealed she had been cutting herself. The underside of her left arm had been viciously and repeatedly cut over and over and over again. I had never seen anything quite like it.

I looked at her and said, "Megan, why do you cut yourself?"

She answered with an honest assessment of her actions. "I cut myself to stop the pain."

In that moment her response did not make sense to me. My mind could not find a rational connection between a person cutting themselves, causing themselves pain, and a hurt-filled, destructive action somehow stopping the pain— though this is the only response I've ever been given on the topic.

It did not then and did not for many years after seem right to me. Then one day, while talking with God in prayer, I began to get some insight into what was being said, a revelation that included how often hurting people hurt people. And more times than not, the people they hurt are themselves.

Today, wherever we can go with our message of hope— high schools, teen challenge centers, convention centers, juvenile detention centers—almost without fail, I share Megan's story and how her life has so affected mine. And every time I tell her story I watch as, predominantly the girls, nod their heads that they know exactly what Megan was describing to me. My guess is they have no idea they are even nodding. The experience is so deeply rooted in their hearts.

As I listened, Megan shared more of her story with me. And then she stopped. She asked if she could give me something from her book bag. I nodded and she pulled out a bloodstained razor blade she had been using to slice open her skin.

A gentle smile came across her face. "Mr. Dean, I no longer want to hurt myself. Can I give this to you?"

I opened my hand, and she carefully placed the razor blade in it. Today, after all these years, that razor blade is still with me. I take it with me wherever we go in our travels to speak to teens, because it serves as a very powerful, visual reminder of the choice to believe your life has value and that harming yourself is never the answer.

NOT JUST RAZOR BLADES

Sadly, the story of self-harm does not end there. After I had finished speaking at another high school, I felt like the message had fallen flat. There had been no audible or visible response. As the students quietly and orderly left the auditorium, the principal and I talked. He graciously shared with me how much our message had meant to him and to his students.

Though I had felt no real emotional connection, hearing his thoughts was helpful as this is what gets us out of bed every morning, knowing there are teenagers, just like you, across the country and around the world who are likewise waking up, but doing so with absolutely no hope in their lives. They have somehow become convinced their lives do not matter. But there is always hope! How do I know? Because God woke them up.

I shook hands with the principal and began to walk with my road manager toward the front lobby. Approaching us from the opposite direction was a young man who seemed to be carrying a heavy emotional load. It was clear he was not going to let us out of his sight before sharing what was weighing so heavily on him.

Looking straight at us, Thomas extended a hand and said hello. As we shook hands, he said, "Thank you for coming to my school today. Thank you for telling me that my life matters. I want to give you something."

With that, Thomas pulled a cigarette lighter out of his jacket. As he tried to hand it to me, I said, "Thomas, thank you for this, but I do not smoke."

He quickly responded, "I don't smoke either. I use the lighter to burn myself when I want to stop the pain."

It was exactly what every teenager has said to me when we've talked about their reasons for self-harm: "I hurt myself to stop the pain."

Once again I was dumbfounded. Not just by the way God allowed me to see that He always uses our obedience to Him, whether we see it or know it or not, but how quickly God can change a heart.

I thanked Thomas for his "gift" and affirmed him in the decision he had made. A small smile slid across his face as he walked away. The undeniable heaviness he'd walked up with just moments before was now gone.

WHEN OTHERS HURT US

Within a few short minutes of finishing up a Sunday morning service where I'd spoken about forgiveness, Chip, a young man in his late teens, asked to talk to me. The look on his face told me he didn't want to talk, but he desperately needed to be heard.

We shook hands and I asked him to share whatever was on his heart. Chip said that what I had shared about having been sexually abused as a fifteen-year-old was something he could relate to. His eyes then shifted from me to the floor and then back to me. He said, "What happened to you when you were fifteen happened to me when I was twelve."

The pain from that experience was still very evident both on his face and in the tone of his voice. He went on to say he didn't understand why he needed to forgive someone who had hurt him. After all, he was just a kid when he had been abused.

My abuse at fifteen was in essence thirty-six months after his, at age twelve, so we had something in common. It helped bind us together in a brotherhood of sorts—one in which no one willingly desires membership.

I talked with Chip about the destructive cycles that take root in our hearts when we have been hurt by others and refuse to let that hurt go. Not to excuse or ignore wrongful actions, but to choose to forgive.

I told him, "God created us with the ability to make choices. Choices create circumstances. Good choices produce good circumstances and, likewise, bad choices create bad circumstances. When others hurt us, that is never acceptable. It is wrong. What makes the difference is how we respond to that hurt. It goes a long way in determining the future us."

The same is true for you.

WHY DO WE HURT OURSELVES?

From a young girl's razor blade in Texas to an encounter with a young man and a cigarette lighter comes the question, "Why do we hurt ourselves?" I'm glad you asked! One of the primary reasons I've heard, and have come to better understand, is that when someone hurts themselves, they do so in an attempt to stop or at least overpower the emotional pain they are feeling. But they also do it because it's one area of their life where they feel they have some control. And control of our lives is something so many of us spend so much time trying to stay on top of.

Frankly, self-harm is a sign of extreme distress. If you are doing this, or you know someone who is, please seek professional help, because self-harm is not the answer. It doesn't fix anything; in fact, it makes things worse.

I'm sure you've been in the emergency room or a doctor's office and been asked to rate your pain on a scale from one to ten. Number one indicates no real, discernable pain, and ten is the worst pain you've ever felt. That works for physical pain but unfortunately not for emotional pain. It hurts in ways and depths that cannot be measured.

It's when you know, for sure, everything's not fine.

WHAT ABOUT YOU?

It's time to get personal. You may be the only person who knows you've been hurt by someone, as in abused physically or mentally. Or that you've been hurting yourself.

The thing is you shouldn't keep it to yourself! You may not have considered this, but holding it in increases the pain.

So be kind to yourself. Find a professional or a trusted family member or friend and share your pain with them. First, it will help diminish your pain significantly. And second, it will get you started on a path to healing.

Do it. You deserve to be pain free!

TRUTH FROM THE CHAPTER

Let's recap a few of the truths from this chapter to think about and to remember:

- Hurting people hurt people. And more times than not, the people they hurt are themselves.
- There is always hope! How do we know? Because God woke us up.
- Whether we see it or not, God uses our obedience to Him.
- Destructive cycles can take root in our hearts when we've been hurt by others and then refuse to let the hurt go.
- God created us with the ability to make choices that go on to create circumstances.
- Self-harm is never the answer. It doesn't fix anything; in fact, it makes things worse.
- You deserve to be pain free!

TRUTH FROM GOD'S WORD

You should know that your body is a temple for the Holy Spirit who is in you. You have received the Holy Spirit from God. So you do not belong to yourselves, because you were bought by God for a price. So honor God with your bodies.

(1 Cor. 6:19–20)

"I say this because I know what I am planning for you," says the LORD. "I have good plans for you, not plans to hurt you. I will give you hope and a good future."

(Jer. 29:11)

MY PRAYER FOR YOU

Father, today we need Your help to understand once again how much we are loved by You. Help us to receive the truth that You created us on purpose. That it wasn't an accident. That there was a reason, and that You want to use us in the world around us. Help us to embrace the truth that everything You do is intentional and right. We take a deep breath as we work to stop buying the lie that hurting ourselves stops pain. We now know the truth and it will set us free! In Jesus' name. Amen.

In the space that follows, or in a separate journal, write the answers to these questions. Since this is your story be honest with yourself. It's the only way to truly change your life forever!

Have you ever hurt yourself to stop the pain?

_____

_____

_____

_____

_____

_____

_____

_____

Have you ever wondered why the pain is in your life and maybe what is the origin of the pain? Write about it in the space below.

_____

_____

_____

_____

_____

_____

_____

Do you understand two negatives do not make a positive? Meaning, hurting yourself to stop pain never works. In your own words, write what you're feeling right now.

_____

_____

_____

_____

_____

_____

_____

_____

_____

_____

_____

CHAPTER 5

Afraid to Go to School

The headlines were everywhere with the horrific news: three students had been killed and five were wounded at a school shooting in December 1997 in the small rural town of West Paducah, Kentucky. What began as a normal school day the Monday after Thanksgiving turned to tragedy when a fourteen-year-old freshman unleashed unthinkable evil on his classmates. Sentenced to life in prison and denied his one chance for parole at twenty-five years, he will spend the rest of his life regretting his decision.

At 7:30 a.m. on that December 1st, as they did every morning prior to the start of the school day, thirty-five students came together in the front lobby of Heath High School to pray. As they stood in a circle, holding hands, singing songs, and talking to God, unnoticed and off to the side was a young man standing by himself. By all accounts he had come to school that morning with a demonic mission and an arsenal of weapons—a pistol, loaded clips, shotgun shells, hundreds of bullets, and two shotguns and two rifles wrapped in a blanket.[1] He had told his sister the blanket contained a school project.

Eyewitnesses reported that as the group finished their prayers, Michael Carneal calmly put earplugs in his ears and pulled out a handgun. Assuming a firing position, and without any warning, he opened fire. As the bullets torpedoed out of the gun, students were hit one by one and fell to the ground. The first bullet struck Missy Jenkins, a popular fourteen-year-old freshman.[2]

When he heard the unmistakable sound of gunfire, principal Bill Bond rushed out of his office to see what was happening. The leader of the prayer group called the gunman by name and shouted, "What are you doing? Put the gun down!"

Unfazed, Michael continued to pull the trigger.

More students fell with every shot fired.

In all of the horror and confusion, Michael stopped to reload his weapon. At that moment, Principal Bond moved into an open space in the hallway, placing himself in the line of fire. When he did this, Michael put down his gun and surrendered.

As quickly as it began, it was over. Of the eleven shots fired, eight had found their mark. Three girls were dead— seventeen-year-old Jessica James, fourteen-year-old Nicole Hadley, and fifteen-year-old Kayce Steger (who had dreamed of one day being a police officer)—and five other students were wounded.

IS IT GETTING WORSE?

The first documented shooting at a U.S. schoolhouse occurred in 1853 in Louisville, Kentucky.[3] For the next 125 years, school shootings were rare. Then, in the late 1980s to the early 1990s, there was a sharp increase.[4]

Not all shootings made the headlines. Those that did were in Paducah in 1997; Jonesboro, Arkansas, in 1998; and in Littleton, Colorado in 1999. The 1999 shooting occurred at Columbine High School, which, at the time, because of the number killed (thirteen—fifteen if you include the shooters) was the worst mass shooting at a school in the nation's history. Columbine, however, now ranks fourth, behind Sandy Hook Elementary in Newtown, Connecticut, in 2012 (28 fatalities); Robb Elementary School in Uvalde, Texas, in 2022 (22); and Marjory Stoneman Douglas High School in Parkland, Florida, in 2018 (17).

Today, school shootings are becoming tragically common. David Riedman, the founder and independent researcher of the K–12 School Shooting Database, has collected statistics dating back to 1966 that show how shootings have increased over time and dramatically over the last six years. In his study there are an unbelievable 2,761 incidents with 2,246 victims wounded, 818 victims killed, and 1,066 deaths (including the shooters).[5]

Another study reports that, since 1999, 338,000 students have experienced gun violence at school, with 2022 resulting in the highest number ever at 304 incidents.[6] But in

2023 there were 346 shooting incidents across the country, resulting in 248 victims being either wounded or killed, not including the shooter(s)—now the highest yearly total since 1966.[7]

Prior to 2018 the number of incidents had never reached sixty in any given year, and totals in the fifties were uncommon. But the number of incidents in 2023 was nearly six times that threshold, with 2018 and 2021 both seeing notable spikes with the number of incidents doubling year over year.

Unfortunately, the tally continues to climb.

BACK TO PADUCAH

The evening of the 1997 Paducah shooting, my wife, Lori, and I were at home when we saw the news of the three students who were killed and the five who were wounded. I found myself immediately drawn to the students in the report. Their faces were marked by fear from the violence and devastation they had just experienced. So many lives would never be the same!

Sitting in our family room that December evening I vividly remember feeling that one day I would go to this school and share my heart with those affected. It was nineteen months later when I would be invited to be part of a week-long program called "Rising to the Challenge." In September the You Matter ministry team headed to Paducah to share our message of hope with the students at that campus.

The day before I was scheduled to speak, I talked to Pam, one of the ladies on staff at the high school who had invested a lot of time in developing the program we were now only hours away from kicking off. I asked her if any local media would be covering the event. Pam confirmed the local newspaper was indeed covering it and that a national news crew was already on-site.

That night, after checking into our hotel, Lori and I headed to dinner. Neither of us knew what to expect the next morning. All we knew for sure was that God had sent us to this school and that He had a special plan for this event and these students. But what would He have me share with them? I desperately needed God's guidance, direction, and presence.

Later that night, unable to sleep, I got out of bed and walked out onto the porch that overlooked a river. As I stood there in the pitch black of night, I felt the weight of the darkness that had invaded the lives of these students and their families. They had experienced something and, as a result, been changed forever. They needed hope!

As I watched the sun rise on the eastern horizon, I was reminded of the power of light in a dark place and that what I would be bringing to the assembly was the hope of Jesus, the absolute Light of the World! The One who came to stamp out darkness forever! A couple of minutes later, Lori joined me on the porch, and together we watched as a new day began to take shape.

Driving through the countryside of this small town in western Kentucky on our way to the school, it was impossible to miss the uniqueness of where we were. Barns, hayfields, cattle, and farmhouses were all we could see as we drove the country roads.

Around a corner and across the railroad tracks we suddenly came face-to-face with the school we had seen on television many months before. As we walked across the parking lot, we knew each step drew us closer and closer to moments God had established since the foundation of time.

Walking into the front lobby of the school, we stepped into the chaos that oftentimes accompanies the beginning of a school day. We walked beside clusters of young people and then amid a few television crews who were canvassing the halls. Making our way down a corridor, we entered a room that was filling up with teachers, local officials, and volunteers.

FACING FEAR

When the first bell rang and the students settled into their homerooms, I found myself feeling drawn back down the long hallway toward the front lobby. Just before crossing the threshold, I couldn't help but notice that I was by myself. Just me and the memories of what had happened here on that cold, horrific morning just months ago.

For the first time since receiving the invitation to come to the school, the reality of my surroundings crashed over me. Standing in that lobby, where an assault of evil had been launched, my thoughts rushed to the individuals who had been most affected by the events of that day, thinking about the fear that must have gripped them. I remembered what Principal Bill Bond had said afterward. Because there is no manual for these scenarios, he knew it was up to him to determine how they handled things. He decided to bring the students back the very next day, saying, "If we had closed the school, it would have been for only one reason, fear. And it would have put the shooter in charge, and I didn't want him to be in charge."[8]

Walking around the lobby, reflecting on that day and thinking about this day, I was reminded of what the Bible says in Ephesians 6:13 (NIV): "Therefore put on the full armor of God, so that when the day of evil comes, you may be able to stand your ground, and after you have done everything, to stand."

The armor of God! We do not need to fear! We simply need to suit up (prepare) and then stand on God's promise to care for and protect us!

I stood in silence for a few minutes as I thanked God for the reminder and for the four verses that follow with the description of God's armor: the belt of *truth*, the breastplate of *righteousness* (which is being and living right in the eyes of God), the shoes of the gospel of *peace*, the shield of *faith*, the helmet of *salvation*, and the sword of the Spirit, which is God's Word, the *Bible*.

My moment of silence came to an abrupt halt as the shrill sound of the bell signaled the end of the first period and launched a sudden surge of students from all directions as they filed out of the classrooms and into the hallways that led to the auditorium. I went back into the room where the administrators and guests had gathered, and we prepared to enter the auditorium that was now full with the entire student body. Lori was escorted to a seat. I placed myself in the back of the auditorium, leaning against the wall, taking it all in as I watched students positioning themselves for a program that had been in the planning stage for at least six months. I watched, listened, and mostly prayed.

LOOKING FORWARD, NOT BACKWARD

As I prayed, I sensed a direction that surprised me: to not mention the shooting, not even allude to it, but instead to talk about having a vision for the future. After all, hope doesn't change the past; hope is always for now and for tomorrow.

I struggled with the thought of not mentioning the shooting because, after all, that's what brought me here. How could I let these students know that those who were still suffering from the gunshots and indeed those who had lost their lives were not forgotten? With my thoughts spinning, I began to wonder what would and could I say that had not already been said before. I realized I was beginning to let the pressure of the moment take over. That's when God's Spirit reminded me that He was with me and He would stay with me when I began to speak. My job was to trust Him and His Word: "Forgetting the past and straining toward what is ahead, I keep trying to reach the goal and get the prize for which God called me through Christ to the life above" (Phil. 3:13b–14). Why spend your energy looking back when you have an incredible future to come that will bring you hope, not fear, as well as the ultimate prize of life with God?

So that's what I did. I took a step back and gave God the space He needed to do His work, without me in the way. I very simply shared these two truths based on His Word.

- Don't let your past rob you of your future; hope is on the horizon. (Col. 3:1–4)
- Yesterday ended last night. Tomorrow is promised to no one. So we've been given this gift called today. (Phil. 3:13b–14; Ps. 103:15–18)

And with these two points in mind, hope—the real kind of hope based on God's truth—was offered to and reso-nated with the students.

I paused for a moment, with the doors to the auditorium open and a large-blade fan pulling the hot August air of western Kentucky into the auditorium, and took one last all-consuming look at the students, faculty, and staff.

"Learn from your past, plan for your future, and live today to its maximum potential," I said. "I believe in you! God bless you."

With that, the assembly was over.

WAS ANYONE THERE THAT DAY?

As the students filed out of the auditorium, many stopped to say thanks. I walked over to a couple of teachers and listened as they shared their thoughts with me. And because it had been nearly two years since the shooting, I found myself asking if anyone in attendance had been at the school when the tragedy had occurred. One of the teachers responded that many of them had been here that day. And three of the five students who had been wounded were here today as well! That's when Lori and I asked if we could meet Missy Jenkins.

Moments later, seated in a wheelchair with a smile that lit up the room, Missy came toward us. What Lori and I noticed first and foremost was that God's love was clearly evident in her face and behaviors. She showed no bitterness for where she was in life and never once during our conversation wandered toward a pity party or the inevitable question that most people in her position might have asked: Why me?

As the three of us talked, Missy shared some of her plans for the immediate future. We even discussed the possibilities of speaking together at a few assemblies and church youth events at some point in the future.

How could Missy not be resentful but instead be upbeat, all while being bound to a wheelchair? The secret lies in something she said in a 2022 CBN interview: "There were two roads I could have taken: there was a road to be angry about the whole situation and to feel negative about the situation and feel that nothing will get any better or the other road that I'm doing now is to be happy and to live my life and to have a family. And I thank God so much for showing me the right road and to remind me that I can still do anything that I want to, even though I'm in a wheelchair—that my life isn't over. I have a purpose in my life and I consider myself very blessed to be able to know that!"[9]

Instead of anger, bitterness, and thoughts of revenge, Missy chose to obey God's instructions from Luke 6:27–28, which tells us to love our enemies, do good to those who hate us, bless those who curse us, and pray for those who mistreat us. But none of that can be done if we haven't forgiven the person, that "enemy" who caused us pain in the first place.

And don't think Missy was just unique or special in her ability to do this—no one can forgive another, especially with something as devastating as these circumstances. It is humanly impossible—except for the work of God and His help through the power of His Spirit that's available to everyone.

Missy ended her CBN interview by saying: "I think the only explanation I can give is that God gave me the ability to forgive."

I am so grateful to have met Missy. She has the heart of a champion in that she is willing to do what so many others would not! But she also displays the determined resolve to become all that she was created to be.

MORE THAN SHOOTINGS

School violence is more than shootings. Not everyone uses a gun, knife, or some other weapon to exact their anger on others. For instance, because of the high levels of anxiety, fear, and chaos, especially after the COVID-19 lockdown, many *false* reports of suspected shootings emerged (commonly called swatting). In fact, false reports of active shooters were the most common violent incident during the 2022–2023 school year.[10] While these incidents might be thought of as just a threat, they have a significant impact in that they traumatize students and staff, waste emergency response resources, and undermine the feeling of safety and security needed for schools to function effectively.

Then there is the issue of bullying—what I experienced during my time in school that is now reaching epidemic proportions. The statistics are staggering. And scary. Here are just a few facts published in January 2024:

- 90% of students in grades 4 to 8 report having been harassed or bullied.
- 28% of students in grades 6 to 12 experience bullying.

- Over 160,000 kids refuse to go to school each day for fear of being bullied. (National Education Association)
- 70.6% of students report having witnessed bullying in their school—and over 71% say bullying is a problem.
- Each month 282,000 students are physically assaulted in some way in secondary schools throughout the United States—and the number is growing.
- 86% of students surveyed said, "other kids picking on them, making fun of them or bullying them" is the number one reason that teenagers turn to lethal violence at school.
- 64% of students who are bullied do not report it. (Petrosina, Guckenburg, Devoe and Hanson 2010)[10]

This begs the question, What can we do?

Besides legislation to establish anti-bullying policies and laws so there are consequences for this behavior, it's going to take awareness, training (of staff, students, and parents), and intervention. This will require empowering both those in authority and those being targeted to address the situation firmly but calmly. But it also means we need the love of God and His help with all of this, including forgiveness of those who do the bullying. Their behaviors—most always the result of their own insecurities, perceptions of powerlessness, and need for control—have hijacked their souls.

Clearly, everything's *not* fine.

Walking back to our vehicle after the Heath High School assembly, Lori and I stopped at the main entrance and silently looked at the memorial marker that today sits adjacent to the school's front door. The high school graduated its last class in 2013, fifteen years after the shooting. While there was talk of closing the school, the high school was instead merged with two others, and the school buildings are now home to middle schoolers, students who have never heard people talk about the infamous shooting (unless they wanted to know more about the marker at the school entrance). This is proof that life moves on, and our best way forward is to move with it.[11]

Driving away, I took one final glance in my rearview mirror and saw the bright sunshine atop the building where earlier the forces of good and evil had battled. As the school disappeared from view, I felt a knowing in my heart that the people at this school had surely navigated the hope-filled journey from tragedy to triumph.

WHAT ABOUT YOU?

With school violence so often in the news, it's hard to not walk around in fear and/or anger at what is happening. But remember, how you respond to something determines how much control that something has in your life. It's also worth noting that fear never comes from God. He did not give us fear, but He did give us love, power, and a sound and disciplined mind.

Anger is an emotion that requires our attention. Did you know that even Jesus became angry? He did! But He did not sin in that anger. He was under such control of His emotions that He simply refused to give in to the temptation that precedes our sinning. He did this not just because He's God, but because He was fully yielded to God. You and I can do the very same thing.

What do you do when you become angry? How do you process that emotion? Knowing how to recognize and diffuse situations that cause anger to rise from deep within your heart is essential. So is learning how to refuse to allow fear to take up residence in your life.

And for those of you who have been bullied, or maybe you find yourself counted among the bullies, I pray that you, too, will discover how much you matter!

TRUTH FROM THE CHAPTER

Let's recap a few of the truths from this chapter to internalize and remember.

- In a world filled with violence and uncertainty, it's easy to fall into a pattern of fear. But God tells us we do not need to fear but should instead suit up with the armor He tells us about in Ephesians 6:13.
- After we prepare ourselves with God's armor— *truth, righteousness, peace, faith, salvation,* and the

Bible—we need only to stand there, on His promises, knowing that He cares for us and protects us.

- Why do bad things happen to good people? The short answer is because we live in a world that, in the garden of Eden, was given over to Satan's influence. His mission statement has always been "to steal and kill and *destroy*" (John 10:10 emphasis added). But that verse does not stop with the word destroy. It goes on to say that Jesus has come to bring us life in the fullest sense possible!

TRUTH FROM GOD'S WORD

Where God's love is, there is no fear, because God's perfect love drives out fear.

(1 John 4:18a)

My dear friends, don't try to get even. Leave room for God to show his anger. It is written, "I am the God who judges people. I will pay them back," says the Lord.

(Rom. 12:19 NIRV)

MY PRAYER FOR YOU

Today, as I pray, I ask Jesus that You give us the deep, deep assurance that You are the only One who can provide all we need in the face of fear and anxiety. Remind us that You are our shield and that You will fight for us, but also that You know what it's like to be bullied, to suffer, even to the point of having experienced a cruel and undeserved death. And for the ones who are hurting others because of their own pain and insecurities, bring Your light and healing to them. In Your name I pray. Amen.

In the space that follows, or in a separate journal, write the answers to these questions. Since this is your story be honest with yourself. It's the only way to truly change your life forever!

Are you fearful of the what-ifs of life? If so, what does God offer that can help you change this?

_____

_____

_____

_____

Have you ever been bullied or bullied someone else? If so, recap the instance(s) here.

_____

_____

_____

_____

How do you respond when something angers you? Consider writing down your emotions instead of acting them out. Then find someone you trust who you can talk to.

CHAPTER 6

_____

_____

_____

_____

You've Messed Up, Again

Have you ever been inside a prison? Ever had to clear six levels of intense security to get to where you're going? Ever walked into a room filled to capacity with teenagers who were locked up for very serious crimes? Ever felt as if all eyes were laser-focused on you, and you actually sensed their two questions: Who is this guy? Why is he here?

It was Christmas Eve, and as has been my habit every year since 1994, I was visiting a juvenile detention center to share a message of hope with the teenagers who are locked up. These kids are not in prison for petty offenses, such as chewing gum in class or for running in school halls. They're not locked up because their parents could not control their actions. No, they are behind bars for committing serious crimes, ranging from burglary to gang violence to murder.

This morning was especially cold and harsh. The welcoming committee consisted of razor-wire fencing and security cameras. To add to the dreariness, the parking lot was empty, the concrete was wet because it had rained the night before, and the wind was howling. Having spoken at this place many times before, I was very familiar with the procedure: walk to a side gate, push a button, look northward into the sky so one of the security cameras positioned on a nearby pole can identify who is requesting access to the building.

As the electronic doors swung open, I walked in. With each step I moved closer and closer to the God-given opportunity to share hope with some teens who are at the lowest level of human existence.

After my identity was verified, I heard the unmistakable, unforgettable sound of heavy prison doors unlocking and opening and then closing and locking again behind me. From there I was taken to a classroom where twenty-seven teens were seated at school desks—nineteen young men and eight young ladies who were spending Christmas in prison.

I thanked them for the opportunity to share a few minutes of their lives with them and then dove right into how their incarceration affected them by asking a simple question: How does your family feel about where you are today? At first, they were leery of answering. But as is the case almost every time I speak in a prison, one person exhibits some leadership qualities by answering. Today, it was a young man to my right. His response was short and to the point.

"My parents are sad that I'm here," he said.

Off to my left a young lady said, "My family doesn't care that I'm here."

Finally, from the back of the room came the answer that most shocked me. It was from a young man who said, "No one in my family even knows that I'm here."

As I thought about those three answers, I wondered about the remainder of the teens who had not yet vocalized their responses. What were their answers? What was it like to already be serving time for serious crimes at their young age?

I then asked how many of them had been locked up more than once, and twenty-six of the twenty-seven raised their hands. What was causing them to make one bad choice after another? Choices that led them straight into the painful and demoralizing cycle of breaking the law and then serving time for their actions. I knew if they could get even a small glimpse of their personal value and begin to recognize the potential they had been given by the Creator of the universe, then they would most likely never choose to break the law again.

DREAM BIG, DREAM SPECIFIC

About halfway through our time together, I asked the twenty-seven inmates what their dreams were. I ask this question almost every time because I've learned the power of dreaming. Still, you might be wondering why I would ask this of someone in prison. As a friend once told me, "If the dream is big enough, the facts don't count."

In the book of Proverbs in the Bible—a book that serves as a great guide to living with wisdom—we learn, "Where there is no vision, the people perish" (Prov. 29:18a KJV). Think of it this way, when people have a God-designed vision for their life, they *don't* perish, they live! I'd go so far as to say they come alive in the same way a seed in the ground pushes up out of the dirt and grows into a healthy, flourishing plant.

Having specific goals, dreams, and ambitions for our lives is so very important, because it is in the details of those dreams that we begin to see a plan develop that launches in our heart and plays out in our daily lives. Or as I like to say, nothing in life will ever become dynamic until it first becomes specific.

This discussion about dreams and aspirations leads us to a question: "What is your definition of the word *potential*?" After a few responses such as "being able to do stuff" and "having an opportunity and someone to help me," I asked another question that over the years has resulted in answers as wide-ranging as the people I've asked: "Where would we find the most unused potential in the world?"

It's common in these settings to hear "in prison," but my answer is always "in a cemetery." Think about it. Every book that was never written is dead and buried. Every song that was never recorded is dead and buried. Every "I love you" that was never spoken is dead and buried. In the same way, our God-given potential and calling on our lives is dead and buried when we are no longer alive on Planet Earth. But until then? It's available! Ready, willing, and waiting to be directed and applied.

THE ARTIST

Throughout the conversation about the power of dreams and potential, the teen prisoners became more and more engaged. What a delight, joy, and absolute treasure it was to see a spark of hope being ignited in many of their hearts!

Meanwhile, seated on the very back row, was Joey. He refused to make eye contact or get involved in any way. He seemed totally bored by the conversation and clearly was not happy to be sitting in an assembly on Christmas Eve.

It was so obvious one of the guards in the room asked me, "Do you see the artwork on the walls of this room?" He paused briefly as I looked around the room. Then he said, "The young man who will not speak to you is the artist."

I honestly could not believe what I heard. Immediately, I thought, *What? He's the artist? He doesn't look like an artist.*

In that moment I felt a deep pain in my heart. Without the slightest hesitation I had judged him. Was it based on his potential? No. It was based solely on his appearance, actions, and circumstances. But I was dead wrong.

I took a moment to repent and recover and then looked at Joey and asked, "Is this your artwork?"

He ever so slightly lifted his head and mumbled, "Yep."

The many pieces of art scattered around the room were portraits of prisoners. There was no doubt he was talented.

I said, "You have a real gift from God."

Again, his response was one word, "Yep."

So I asked him, "What are you going to do with what you have been given?"

Once again he shut down.

That's when I heard God quietly speaking to my heart, *I want you to take him outside and talk with him, just the two of you.*

I asked the guard, "Would you allow Joey and me to go to the cafeteria, where you can see us, and have a few minutes to talk together?"

The guard seemed confused by my question and intentions, because his answer was immediate and unsupportive: "It's his choice if he wants to go with you or not, but if he does choose to go, we are not responsible for what happens."

Because of where we were, the guard's response did not include or incite one shred of comfort. Still, I could not ignore the prompting I had felt only seconds before. I looked directly at the young man and asked him, "Would you go out of this room and talk with me for a few minutes in private, please?"

He stood up and for the first time that morning spoke a complete sentence. "Yeah, I'll go talk with you. Let's go."

As he stood up, fear gripped me. He was massive! I uttered a silent prayer, hoping he was a gentle giant, and then motioned to him to walk in front of me to the cafeteria. Between the classroom and the cafeteria was a glass partition. As I chatted with this young giant of an incarcerated artist, everyone in the classroom watched us through the glass.

I looked up at Joey as he looked down at me.

I extended my hand and we shook hands.

That's when I heard four words I believe God was asking me to say to him. So I said, "I believe in you."

In that instant, this teen, the largest, toughest inmate in the prison, began to cry.

"How can you believe in me?" he asked. "You don't even know me."

My response was simple and to the point. "I believe in you because you are breathing."

And with that conversation, we went back to the classroom.

LOCKED UP

When I speak in prisons, I often share with the teen inmates that many people on the outside of the prison walls are more locked up than they are on the inside. Let's identify the two ways this plays out and if you might be able to relate to either of them.

I Have No Value

One of the ways people live in their own private prison is through living life every day consumed with worrying about what other people think about them. They find their value, or at least their perceived value, based on the opinions of others rather than on the truth of how valuable each of them truly is. Maybe you find yourself within this group. You are really struggling and deeply fearful of being judged. If so, maybe it will help you to know that you are not alone.

Whenever I wrestle with a question about something, I have found the best source for a trustworthy answer is to search out God's opinion on the matter. Especially when it comes to my value as a human being. Why not look to Who created me? Not my parents, but God Himself. Check this out. In chapter 3 we referenced Psalm 139:4, but let's read it again with the verses that surround it. "You made my whole being; you formed me in my mother's body. I praise you because you made me in an amazing and wonderful way. What you have done is wonderful. I know this very well. You saw my bones being formed as I took shape in my mother's body. When I was put together there, you saw my body as it was formed. All the days planned for me were written in your book before I was one day old" (vv. 13–16).

The answer to the question of whether you have any value is simply this: God says you are amazing and wonderful! From the very beginning of your existence, and not dependent on anything you've said or done, but simply because He created you with worth, a plan, and purpose.

You Have No Value

Maybe, like me, you have judged someone else regarding their worth, usefulness, significance, and value. And maybe, like me, you've realized what you did was wrong. Again, looking to God's Word, we learn that if we judge, we will be judged. In fact, it tells us we will be judged in the same way we judge others (Matt. 7:1–2)!

It's easy to see all the imperfections and mess ups in someone else's life, but the truth is we all have them. No one is perfect. We are each the result of our past experiences, both good and bad, which causes us to see life differently but also to respond differently.

Judging says more about us than the other person, so don't fall into the trap of judging someone else and their value. That's God's job.

SO WHAT DO WE DO?

One of the coolest things any of us can do as far as being critical of others is to consider being a voice of hope for someone who has felt, or today feels, judged.

We talked about bullying in the previous chapter and how it often stems from one's own low self-esteem and feelings of worthlessness. We compensate by projecting ourselves as superior. Think about it this way. Bullying is as harmful to the bully as it is to the one being bullied. No one wins.

The truth is you have a choice.

When life is difficult, and you're overwhelmed with the feeling that everything's not fine, one sympathetic voice, one kind gesture may very well be the bridge that gaps feeling hopeless and finding the hope to hang on to the belief that life is going to get better. So be that voice, either to yourself or to someone else.

It was now time to leave the prison. I walked out of the classroom, back through all the very tight security checkpoints, back out into the cold, and back through the gate that has, as a visual reminder of where I've been, rolls of razor wire that completely encompass the facility. I turn and take a long look over my shoulder at the building I have just come out of, knowing that inside are twenty-seven teenagers who will be locked up on Christmas morning. But maybe, just maybe, the hope we had been able to extend to them will give their faith what it needs to make it through the next day and move forward in life, knowing that God loves them, that there is a plan for their lives, and that their lives really do matter.

WHAT ABOUT YOU?

Maybe you're not in prison as you're reading this book or listening to the audio version. At least not a physical prison. But maybe, like so many teens I've met here in the United

States and around the world, you know what it's like to be locked up in an emotional or even spiritual prison, where you can't seem to break free from feeling like you're not enough or that God doesn't love you or your life doesn't matter. Sure, everything might seem fine on the outside, but what's really happening on the inside?

It's important to remember this truth: internal reality becomes external reality. What that means is that what's happening on the inside, your thoughts and beliefs, eventually plays out on the outside in your actual life.

I want you to know that I believe in you! I want you to know that you are not alone, that God has a plan and purpose for your life. Please, stay with me to the end of this book, and together we will discover how much you matter!

TRUTH FROM THE CHAPTER

Let's recap a few of the truths from this chapter to internalize and remember.

- Judging others is never a good choice.
- If you do not want to be judged, you shouldn't judge.
- You are not alone; God is always with you.
- Learn to be grateful, even to celebrate what makes you uniquely special.
- Don't quit. Don't give up. God loves you so very much! There is hope! You've just got to choose to believe.

TRUTH FROM GOD'S WORD

Don't judge others, or you will be judged.
(Matt. 7:1)

So if the Son makes you free, you will be truly free.
(John 8:36)

MY PRAYER FOR YOU

Father in heaven, right here, right now, I pray for those who are locked up in a real prison, but also for those who might otherwise be locked up emotionally and spiritually. You tell us in Hebrews 13:8 that You are the same yesterday, today, and forever. This means Your love for us never changes, no matter where we are or what we are doing. Thank You for forgiving all of us for where we have missed the mark and help us today to realize and receive how much we are loved by You. In Jesus' name. Amen.

In the space that follows, or in a separate journal, write the answers to these questions. Since this is your story be honest with yourself. It's the only way to truly change your life forever!

Why do you think people judge each other?

_____

_____

_____

_____

_____

_____

_____

_____

_____

Have you ever judged someone based on their appearance? If so, how did you feel about yourself afterward?

_____

_____

_____

_____

_____

_____

_____

_____

_____

CHAPTER 7

It's Only a Game

Natalie curls her hair and applies thick makeup to cover the many blemishes on her skin. The eyelash extensions cost more than she expected but were totally worth it. At least in her opinion. That and the skinny filter she uses on TikTok should help. But now, what to wear? It's been a few days since her last selfie. For sure she needs to post a new one today. Yeah, it's a lot to keep up with, but without it—she doesn't even want to think about that.

Scrolling through Snapchat, Joe found what he was looking for, but it hurt worse than he thought it would. It was true. Everyone else in the group had been invited except him. How could he face them at school on Monday without it getting weird? Guess he needed to come up with a story he could post that would make them all take more notice of him. But what could it be this time?

Every day in the United States teens average nearly five hours on social media. The apps vary from the most popular, YouTube and TikTok, to Instagram, Facebook, Snapchat, and X (formerly known as Twitter). Five hours every single day. This is far more time than teens spend watching television, doing homework, engaging in hobbies, or playing video games. Why? A 2023 Gallup report says it's for entertainment, communication, and the relief of boredom.[1] Okay, so what's the big deal?

Teens who spend more than five hours a day on social media were 60 percent more likely to express suicidal thoughts or harm themselves. There also are negative views of their body and a struggle with overwhelming sadness. But these effects are small, relative to the decline of overall mental health observed in recent years.

For instance, they use so-called beauty filters—photo-editing tools using AI to alter facial features in photos.[2] Snapchat found that more than 90 percent of teens use filter products on their apps. And more than 600 million people have used these filters on Facebook and Instagram.

Why did they use them? Ninety-four percent reported they felt intense pressure to look a certain way.

Comparing yourself to a perfect image is a no-win battle that causes great suffering while also eroding your self-esteem.

And for those continuously counting their likes, follows, and reposts, let's be very honest with each other: it's a no-win game. It'll never be enough! While there's nothing wrong with wanting to be liked by others, it can quickly become a trap if that is your goal. And quite frankly, if you had an inkling of how very much you are loved by God, then counting likes wouldn't be an issue.

A SUICIDE GAME

Eight days after our ministry received a phone call with a desperate request for help, we were stepping into a scenario where, in two months' time, multiple students attempted to end their lives. Tragically, three had succeeded.

The call was from a Native American tribe with an invitation to speak at every junior and senior high school on its reservation. With some logistical maneuvering, we were on our way to share our message of hope.

What could cause an outbreak of attempted suicides? The answer was a so-called game that was circulating on social media. Sadly, it wasn't a game at all. It was a series of postings on different social media platforms that instructed anyone who cared to watch, not only why ending their life was a desirable option, but also included a graphic guide on how to do so.

When I first heard about the posts, I didn't believe it. There is no way any of the social media platforms would ever allow anything to live online that encouraged someone to commit suicide, much less post instructions on how to do it.

I was wrong.

YOUR LIFE REALLY DOES MATTER

Though social media is supposed to be all about connecting and friendships, anything that is intended for good can be hijacked by evil and used to bring harm.

Over a day and a half, we visited five schools. As I walked into the middle of each gymnasium filled with students, my heart literally hurt. During the conclusion of each assembly, we invited the teens and their families to a mass event scheduled for the evening of the second day. After each of the five assemblies was dismissed, courageous students walked up to share their personal stories, stories that made me tear up. Each time, I asked them, "What could be so bad in your life that you would believe your death would be a better choice than your life?" I'm shocked at how quickly the answers come back, many of which we have addressed in this book.

Every time any of the students realized that we really do care, that we want them to understand and receive the truth that their lives really do matter, I closed my eyes and expressed my gratitude to God. I reminded all of the students that if they were not here, we would all be missing something and someone spectacular. Often that truth alone brings a nod and a smile.

As the time neared for our evening event, it began to rain, which only added to a feeling of gloom. I was concerned about the turnout, but if I've learned anything over the years, it's to trust God for the results He desires and to not worry about things I have no control over.

As I stood by myself on the side of the room to pray, I looked up and saw hundreds of teenagers entering the gym. I watched as they played basketball and ate hot dogs and popcorn. So grateful that they'd all come, I took a panoramic view of the room. A palpable feeling of heaviness settled in. These teens and their families were hurting. They had lost family members, close friends, fellow students. They were confused, their hearts were broken, they needed help, hope, and healing.

After a brief introduction I walked across the gym floor, picked up the microphone, and began to share the message that God loves them so much that He gave up His only Son to die in their place. I revealed some of my personal story and then invited them to make the choice of a lifetime: to ask this same Jesus to come into their life to be in charge and in control. I asked them to raise their hand if they wanted to choose Jesus, and hands went up all over the room! I've done this thousands of times, but each time I get to do it, it's like doing it all over again for the very first time. I felt so excited and grateful because I knew their lives were about to forever change. They were making the most important decision they'd ever make!

As I invited those who had raised their hands to step out from their seats and walk forward to the stage area, I explained that with each step they took toward the front, heaven was taking steps toward them. Because God always meets us where we are and gently leads us to where He desires us to be.

On this night more than seventy teenagers gave their hearts to Jesus! After leading them in a prayer and connecting them with local youth pastors who are part of the team, it was time for our group to leave. Though I was grateful for the victory we saw that night, my heart was still heavy from the deceit of the suicide social media game, and the resulting unnecessary loss of precious lives. I vowed to turn that heaviness into doing whatever I could to stop the evil from continuing.

NOT ALL SOCIAL MEDIA IS BAD

Social media is a great way to connect with people who have hobbies or experiences in common with us. It's helpful for keeping in touch with people who may live far away, for celebrating life events, and to simply bring a smile to your face. But when social media distracts, disrupts, exposes, negatively impacts, and becomes addictive, it takes on a dark, unhealthy, and destructive tone.

We all know there are years and volumes of research linking social media use and abuse to negative effects, including many mental health disorders. What can we do? The better question is what can *you* do?

Don't make your parents do it; take steps to protect yourself! Consider these ideas as a place to begin to limit the negative side effects inherent on all the social media platforms.

- Set rules and limits to help you follow a manageable schedule.
- Ask your parents/guardians or close friends to challenge you to be faithful to your guidelines.

- Use privacy settings.
- Have more face-to-face contact with your friends.

Though it's obvious that everything is not always fine when it comes to social media, let's also recognize that it's not all fun and games and that we each have a choice in how we use it and how we let it affect us. To that end, it's important to set your own personal guidelines so that you'll know if you're in charge of it or if the opposite is true—it's in charge of you.

WHAT ABOUT YOU?

Why do you use social media? Do you find your time on your phone helpful or hurtful? When you put your phone down, are you better informed or are you reeling from hours of watching other people create content they want you to see?

The ultimate question we all need to ask ourselves is this: Does social media help me feel better about myself or does it drive me to a dark and lonely place where I struggle to be satisfied with myself and my life?

What you do with social media determines how it will affect your life. With all my being, I encourage you to make good choices. The future you depends on it!

TRUTH FROM THE CHAPTER

Let's recap a few of the truths from this chapter to internalize and remember.

- Every day in the United States teens average nearly five hours on social media.
- Teens who spend more than five hours a day on social media are 60 percent more likely to express suicidal thoughts or harm themselves.
- Comparing yourself to a perfect image is a no-win battle that causes great suffering while also eroding your self-esteem.
- Though social media is supposed to be all about connecting and friendships, anything that is intended for good can be hijacked by evil and used to bring harm.

TRUTH FROM GOD'S WORD

Through his power all things were made—things in heaven and on earth, things seen and unseen, all powers, authorities, lords, and rulers. All things were made through Christ and for Christ.
(Col. 1:16)

Trust the LORD with all your heart, and don't depend on your own understanding. Remember the LORD in all you do, and he will give you success.
(Prov. 3:5–6)

MY PRAYER FOR YOU

Jesus, today I pray for teenagers who may be feeling convicted in their hearts because they have spent time looking at questionable things online. Make them aware of You and Your presence. Increase their sensitivity to what dishonors You and others. Also be close to anyone who does not yet see their value. I pray for an encounter with You that will help them see through the lies of the Enemy to the truth that they are uniquely created by You and deeply loved by You. I pray this in Your name. Amen.

In the space that follows, or in a separate journal, write the answers to these questions. Since this is your story be honest with yourself. It's the only way to truly change your life forever!

How much time do you spend on social media every day?

_____

_____

_____

_____

_____

_____

_____

Does social media help you become a better person? Does it bring you down?

_____

_____

_____

_____

_____

_____

_____

_____

_____

How might you be able to use social media as a tool for good in the world?

_____

_____

_____

_____

_____

_____

_____

_____

_____

_____

CHAPTER 8

Why Didn't They Want Me?

When I speak at a chapel service in a Christian school, more so than assemblies at public schools, our team will often encounter an unspoken, calloused attitude from the students that screams they are not interested, irrespective of the topic or who's speaking. It's curious that these faith-based organizations have students who are more resistant, but it's true. So often there is an overriding "I've heard it all before" attitude and they are sure the message is not for them, but at least they're out of class for thirty or forty minutes.

Today was no different.

This Monday morning we walked into a school that is a ministry of a local church and had been in existence for quite some time. It was great to see hallways adorned with Scripture verses and other strategic reminders to the students of God's being in their lives.

- "'For I know the plans I have for you,' declares the LORD, 'plans to prosper you and not to harm you, plans to give you hope and a future.'" (Jer. 29:11 NIV)

- "But those who wait on the LORD shall renew their strength." (Isa. 40:31a NKJV)
- "Fear not, for I am with you." (Isa. 41:10a NKJV)
- "Jesus Christ is the same yesterday, today, and forever." (Heb. 13:8 NKJV)

After saying hello to the school principal, my wife and some friends who were hosting us joined me as we were escorted into the assembly hall. There we found 125 students in grades seven through twelve already seated and waiting for us. As we walked in, I saw their heads turn toward us as they looked to see who was going to be speaking at that morning's chapel. Many of them were already tuning out, showing minimal interest in what was about to happen. After all, if you've been to one chapel service, you've been to them all, right?

After calling the students to attention, the principal introduced Lori and me and then issued the familiar warning for them to be on their best behavior. He also encouraged them to really think about what was going to be shared. And after that brief prelude, we began the presentation.

For me it always starts the same, with God reminding me to tell them that I'm not going to talk to them as teenagers, but as people who have the capacity to make choices that can forever change the trajectory of their lives. And despite any preconceived idea they may have brought into the room with them, I'm not there to try and talk them *into* anything; after all, if I could talk them into something, then someone potentially much more effective than me could likewise talk them out of it.

But it was time to share our message of hope.

SHAWNA'S STORY

Within the first five or six minutes it was obvious that God was with us in the room. Obvious because the students began to sit up straighter, tune in, and engage when I asked some questions during my comments. I noticed one particular girl on the front row. She was laser-focused on what was being shared. And as I made eye contact with other students around the assembly hall, several times I noticed tears running down their faces. This was especially true when I touched on the topic of rejection.

As our time was ending, several students made the choice to become Christians, others embraced forgiveness, acceptance was chosen over rejection, and several students said no to suicide.

After the assembly, as the students were leaving, going to their classrooms, Lori and I were saying good-bye to many who were kind enough to meet us at the front of the room to share their thoughts with us. But I kept an eye on the young girl I'll call Shawna, a girl with tears still flowing down her face who had remained seated on the front row. The principal had also seen her and sat down with her, but I knew it was time for me to join them.

At first, Shawna didn't want to talk. But as I began asking her questions about the assembly, she began to open her heart. The more she talked, the more I understood the reasons behind her tears.

Shawna explained that she had been born in another country and had been adopted by a family there. When she was five years old, her adopted dad had taken her on a business trip with him to a major city. In tremendous detail, she recalled facts about the hotel where they spent the night, about the meal they had in the large restaurant inside the hotel, and about the elevator and all the buttons that took her and her dad to the floor where their room was. Then she took a deep breath, wiped some tears away, and began sharing what appeared to be chapter 2 of her story.

When Shawna fell asleep that night in the hotel room with her dad, she never dreamed that when morning came she would wake up to being all alone. She described how she looked in the bathroom, the closet, even under the bed—but her dad was not there. She said she stayed in the room for what seemed to her to be hours, and then she remembered the elevators. Walking out of the bedroom and down the hallway, she eventually found them.

Figuring that the down arrow on the wall would take her down, she pushed that button. When the door opened, she stepped into an overcrowded elevator and found a space to stand. As she looked at the panel of buttons, she remembered all the buttons that could be pushed but noticed that only one had been. It was for the first floor.

When the door opened, so did Shawna's eyes—to a mass of humanity. She recalled that people were everywhere. As she walked into the hotel lobby, her eyes darted from person to person, but she did not see her dad. She went to the gift shop, but he was not there. Making her way back to the restaurant, where hours earlier she had enjoyed such a fun evening with him, she walked from table to table, thinking that he possibly had come downstairs that morning and was having breakfast. Surely, she would find him here. But as fear gripped her heart and reality began to set in, she realized he was not in the restaurant.

Walking past the front desk and the gift shop and through a set of revolving doors, five-year-old Shawna was immediately thrust into another mass of humanity. That morning the sidewalks and streets were bustling with people on their way to work.

Shawna looked deep into my eyes and said, "I stayed in front of that hotel for three days and three nights, waiting for my dad to come back. He never returned for me."

I had absolutely no idea how to respond to what she was saying. By this point in our ministry, I had heard many stories from teens who had opened up and shared with me some of what had transpired in their lives. But never had I heard a story like this. The principal sitting close to her nodded to me, confirming that what she was sharing had really happened.

Shawna explained that as the hours and days passed, she became unbearably hungry and thirsty and had started looking for food and something to drink. As I listened, part of what was so intriguing, painful, and alarming to me was how a five-year-old could go seemingly unnoticed for three full days and nights.

Once again, wiping the tears from her cheeks, Shawna said that somehow someone from a governmental agency found her and put her in their foster child system. Sometime thereafter mercy was extended, love was offered, and Shawna was adopted by an American family who lived in the northwest United States. She began life over again, but what she carried with her was the tragedy that she had experienced in her home country and the deep, deep trauma that came with it, including the need to forgive the adopted father who had abandoned her.

Understanding trauma requires us to fully grasp the reality that what happened to us should never have happened and, conversely, what did not happen that should have happened is real and often debilitating. Years later this dear young girl was sitting on the front row of a school assembly and asking me, "Why was I rejected?"

Lori and I talked more with her until it was time for us to leave. It was obvious that Shawna was in great hands. She was truly loved by the school staff and was very well received by her fellow students and classmates.

BUT GOD

While we were flying back to Tennessee, I settled in my seat, shut my eyes, and began to think about what it must have been like for Shawna. Not just three days and three nights in total isolation, but what she felt after having been so totally rejected by someone who had told her that she was loved and would be cared for.

What came to mind took me back several thousand years ago when a man was likewise rejected, not just by one person, but by society at large. This man was cruelly executed and then spent three days separated from His Father. But much like Shawna, after three days everything changed. How? Death gave way to a bodily resurrection and Jesus came back to life!

You may have heard this story before, but let me explain why it is so important.

God's first two people, Adam and Eve, had everything going for them. There was just one rule: don't eat the fruit on the tree growing in the middle of the garden. No problem, they had plenty of other fruit. They had everything they would ever need. But what is it about something we're *not* supposed to do that tempts us to do it? Both Adam and Eve bit, literally, and sin entered the human race. It also initiated their punishment. They would have to leave Eden as they were now separated from God.

But God! He hadn't created them to live apart from Him. His desire was for companionship *with* them and their children and their children etc., which includes us. To make it right, God provided a fix, a way to connect them and us to Him again. It's why He sent His Son to earth. Jesus' life, but more so His death, is what paid the price that was owed because of Adam's and Eve's disobedience. Today, all we need to do is to accept what God has provided, a gift really, because it doesn't cost us anything but our commitment to Him. When we do, the gap between us is immediately closed, and we are forever united with Him.

What all of this means is that our You Matter message, which brings hope and help for today, is made possible by God Himself! But also it is always available on the other side of any pain you might experience.

WHO NEEDS HOPE?

Every person needs air to breathe and food to eat to keep on living. It's the same with hope. Emotionally we all need hope. Hope empowers. Hope fuels our vision for our future. Hope often takes us from the lowest valley to the highest mountaintop experiences.

At its core, hope is an earnest expectation that something good is going to happen to us and/or for us. And real hope, God's hope, does not disappoint.

I was reminded of this truth when I was reading Romans 5:3–5:

> We also have joy with our troubles, because we know
> that these troubles produce patience. And patience
> produces character, and character produces hope.
> And this hope will never disappoint us, because God
> has poured out his love to fill our hearts. He gave

us his love through the Holy Spirit, whom God has given to us.

Please don't miss what you just read: God's hope will *never* disappoint us! How is that possible? Because God *is* love. And by way of the Holy Spirit, He pours Himself, His love into us to fill our hearts. His love is endless, and this endless love is the foundation of an unshakable hope that is available to you and to me right here, right now.

TWENTY-ONE FAMILIES

A few years later I was at a Christian school in Missouri. We walked into a chapel service to find all the boys seated on one side of the room and all the girls seated on the other. That may be normal in some cultures, but not so much in America today.

After a brief introduction, I began to share what God had put on my heart to tell them that day. Near the end of our time together I shared Shawna's story of her rejection by her adopted dad. I wish you could have seen their faces. Everyone was riveted, spellbound by what they were hearing, not because I am such a powerful speaker, but because of the power contained in the story and in the message.

Again, there was a young girl seated on the front row who was locked in on Shawna's testimony. It was obvious something was happening in her heart. She simply could not control the tears, crying the entire time I told the story of another young girl who had been rejected, abandoned, and left to fend for herself in a hotel.

Toward the end of the chapel service, I again offered the hope found only in the Good News of Jesus and how He came, lived, and died to bring us the one and only answer for all of life's problems.

Immediately after our final prayer I made my way straight across the front of the room and sat down next to Cindy, the student who was crying so many tears. Again, her principal sat with us, consoling her in a way that perhaps only a mom could console a daughter. I asked Cindy what her response had been to the three questions I ask every time I speak: "Has someone really hurt you?" "Do you know the pain of being rejected and abandoned?" "Do you feel like you don't matter?" She and I talked about her responses to each question.

When I asked Cindy why she had cried so much when I talked about rejection and abandonment, her answer was immediate and direct—and shocking! I literally did not know how to respond.

She said, "I cry because I'm eighteen years old and I have been in twenty-one different foster homes. Why did twenty-one families reject me?"

Truly speechless, I prayed and asked God to come into the conversation. And though my actual prayer would not have won any theological awards, it was honest and from my heart. As soon as I said amen to that prayer, a question popped into my head and heart.

I asked Cindy, "Who do you live with now?"

She instantly smiled, began to dry her eyes, and said, "A family adopted me, and I know they love me."

I assured her that the process works. She agreed but her question lingered.

Why was I rejected by twenty-one families?

No doubt Cindy had a lot of issues to work through, as she needed the power of forgiveness to free her from her feelings of rejection. We were able to arrange for some additional help for her, and then I went on to our next event that evening at a Christian convention.

But I'll never leave Cindy and her devastating question behind. In fact, I shared it with the gathering of students at the convention that night and have many times since, including now, in this book. Each time the response is the same: disbelief and an acknowledgment that rejection was and is a big, big deal for teenagers today.

Clearly, everything's not fine.

WHAT ABOUT YOU?

Merriam-Webster's Dictionary defines *abandoned* as "being left without needed protection, care, or support." Dictionary.com tells us that *abandonment* means "an act or instance of leaving a person or thing permanently and completely."

Have you ever felt as if you've been abandoned? Whether by a parent or by the cool kids at school? The world can so easily overlook you as it strives to serve itself.

If so, you can certainly understand and sympathize with so many teenagers across the world who are dealing with this harsh reality. They have been abandoned. But there is hope! Always. God has promised to never leave you or forsake you. He will never abandon you. In fact, He is as close as your next breath.

TRUTH FROM THE CHAPTER

Let's recap a few of the truths from this chapter to internalize and remember.

- Feeling seen, heard, loved, accepted, and cared for are basic human needs.
- Jesus knows what it feels like to be rejected, separated, and abandoned.
- But God, in His love, provides a way for us to be connected to Him!
- God's love is endless, the foundation of an unshakable hope that is freely available to us.
- Hope is essential, and God's hope never disappoints! God's hope empowers us and fuels the vision for our future.

TRUTH FROM GOD'S WORD

He was hated and rejected by people. He had much pain
and suffering. People would not even look at him.
He was hated, and we didn't even notice him.
(Isa. 53:3)

The LORD himself will go before you.
He will be with you; he will not leave you or forget you.
Don't be afraid and don't worry.
(Deut. 31:8)

MY PRAYER FOR YOU

Jesus, You know everything about everyone. That means
You know us better than we know ourselves. Today, I
pray that all eyes will be opened to seeing You and ourselves as You see us. Guide us to receive Your incredible,
life-changing love and fill us with Your hope that will never
disappoint us. Amen.

In the space that follows, or in a separate journal, write
the answers to these questions. Since this is your story be
honest with yourself. It's the only way to truly change your
life forever!

Have you ever been rejected or abandoned? If so, describe the situation and how it made you feel.

_____

_____

_____

_____

_____

_____

_____

_____

_____

If you've experienced the forgiveness, love, and resulting unshakeable hope that comes from a relationship with God, write a thank-you note to Him. If not, then consider taking that step towards Him now! (You'll never be sorry.)

_____

_____

_____

_____

_____

_____

_____

_____

_____

CHAPTER 9

An Unexpected Loss

The day began like most every other day, with sunny skies and the occasional bird chirp. But off in the distance was a cloud. Not the soft, fluffy variety. This one was dark and ominous. In fact, it looked severe. So it wasn't surprising that before long the wind picked up and tree limbs started bending in ways they were never intended to. Then came the rain. Sprinkles turned into big droplets which became a torrential downpour. It was the stuff of every meteorologist's dream and potential nightmare.

The beauty of a storm is that it's temporary. It comes, it does its thing, then it goes. It doesn't last forever. And though there may be some chairs to turn right-side up and limbs to pick up afterward, suddenly the grass looks greener, the air smells fresher, and the sun is shining as brightly as it had been before. Somehow the storm that threatened to cause irreparable damage in the long run made things better. Somehow.

Years ago I read several books by Andy Andrews titled *Storms of Perfection*.[1] In them Andy shares stories and, in some cases, letters he's received from celebrities and politicians who earlier in their lives went through intense and challenging times. In each case these hard times contributed to what ultimately shaped their character and helped them to develop into people of influence.

Over the past year many of the stories I've encountered from teens just like you have dealt with challenges that can best be described as losses. You may be able to relate to one of them. If you do, my prayer is that you will see these storms that blow into your life from a different perspective. Instead of seeing only the destruction they wreak, see them as storms that can lead to the perfection of your character and your life.

SHE ALWAYS LISTENED

Sally began by telling me that her grandmother had died two weeks before and that she was having an especially tough time. She explained that her grandmother had been the anchor of their family. In fact, every Sunday the family all gathered at her grandmother's house for lunch, a ritual Sally looked forward to every week. As they sat around a farm table, eating and talking, Sally said it seemed like time stood still, because her grandmother would always take time to listen to her. It seems Sally's grandmother understood the truth that teenagers do not necessarily want to talk, but they absolutely, positively need to be heard. Sally knew her voice mattered because her grandmother took the time to listen. With her grandmother she felt heard.

She leaned against the stage and cried as she asked, "Who's going to listen to me now?"

That's a legitimate question because everyone wants and needs to be heard. And when the person who is hearing us is no longer with us or is no longer willing to listen, it creates an "everything's not fine" scenario. But here's some good news. God always hears us. He listens. He waits. He's patient. And His love never grows cold or old. Maybe right here, right now, you would consider talking to God, knowing that He loves you more than you can imagine and wants you to be heard.

HE WAS MY BEST FRIEND

I met Travis on a hot afternoon when I spoke to his football team before they hit the field for practice. I noticed he lingered after my talk was over, and I knew he had something to share with me.

We introduced ourselves to each other, but I noticed he was teetering from side to side, obviously nervous about whatever it was he wanted to say. I told him to take his time, that I was happy to listen to whatever he wanted to talk about.

Travis took a deep breath, but try as he might, the tears he was so diligently pushing back suddenly rolled down his face. After wiping them away, he shared that three days earlier his dog, his best friend, had died. Her death was not unexpected; she was eleven years old. But what Travis was not expecting was the pain he felt and the emptiness her loss had created in the center of his heart. After all, he was only six years old when this golden retriever joined the family, and as a seventeen-year-old, Travis did not want to be in uniform in the middle of the field when he actually wanted to cry out his feelings about his dog.

To help Travis navigate some of the pain he was experiencing, I shared some personal stories with him about my family and our dogs. We've had a lot of them. Mostly German shepherds. In fact, just a few months earlier we, too, had struggled with the pain of losing one of our dogs. Lucy was a very special member of the family. She was quirky, and she was a lot of fun. She had a German shepherd bark, the kind that let anyone close by know they were not welcome on our property. Lucy loved to take walks, and she especially loved jumping on the couches in our family room and cuddling up with whoever might be sitting in front of the television.

While I talked, Travis nodded his head, letting me know he fully understood what I was saying.

I think the fact that Travis and I shared a common experience, the loss of a dog who was much more than a dog, who was a member of the family, brought us together in a way that the pain he was feeling was joined with the pain I had felt. Maybe seeing that there was going to be a time in his future when the memory of his dog was not going to be so heartbreaking but would instead be a warm memory that would bring a smile to his face was helpful, allowing him to embrace the truth I shared.

What was that truth? Do not ignore and run from the pain that comes from loss, but instead ask God to allow your heart to process the pain, and in doing so, move you through the stages of grief until you ultimately land in a place of emotional health.

Do you know about the stages of grief? Like many people, Travis was clueless. He had no idea what I was talking about, so I shared with him the model that breaks grief down into five stages that represent the five different emotions we experience when we process our grief. They are denial, anger, bargaining, depression, and ultimately acceptance. There's no standard time frame for each stage. In fact, there's no actual order; you might bounce back and forth between stages for a while. But it's worth whatever it takes to get through to the final stage: acceptance.

I JUST WANT MY FAMILY BACK

Nicole went to a Christian high school where I spoke at a chapel service. When I met her, it was obvious by the way she carried herself that she was a very confident, serious person. She matter-of-factly marched to the front of the auditorium and asked to talk. She was not emotional. There were no tears. In fact, there was very direct communication. Before we began, as is my practice, I asked a staffer at the school to join our conversation. At first, Nicole was not sure why I had done so, but as I explained to her, accountability is a big deal to me. She accepted that and began to talk.

"My mom and dad are getting divorced. Why did God let this happen?"

She then went quiet, waiting for my response. Her hard question allowed me to ask a few questions of my own.

"How do you feel about your parents getting divorced?"

"Are you angry? Are you sad?"

"Do you feel any responsibility for them splitting up?"

As quickly as I asked, she answered, "Yes, I'm sad. My parents are getting divorced. It also frustrates me. And no, I take no responsibility whatsoever for them splitting up. Why should I? I'm not married to either one of them."

Listening to Nicole's answers, but more importantly, listening to the tone with which she answered me, revealed that what Nicole had just said was the result of what she was experiencing in her heart. I call it the fruit of the root.

There are many times when I talk and listen to teenagers that it is obvious we are starting at a surface level. By that I mean we are dealing with the emotions that result from what they are experiencing as opposed to diving deeper and dealing with the root cause that is producing the fruit of the emotions. When we allow ourselves to go deep and get to the root, then what's really going on inside of us can begin to be better understood and ultimately dealt with. Until that deep dive occurs, by default, we are living only with the fruit, which is not a sustainable way of living.

You might remember, if we do not deal with our emotions, our emotions will deal with us.

After explaining all of this to Nicole, I invited her to take a minute and allow herself to feel what was really going on inside of her. I invited her to give herself permission to get to the root cause. The tough exterior with which she had walked up to me only minutes before gave way to a much softer approach.

She said, "I'm just really sad that my family is breaking apart. My heart aches for my mom and I am mad at my dad, but no matter what he has done, he's still my dad. And I love him. I feel guilty for taking sides, but at this point, I just want my life back. I want all the pain to go away. I want to go back to the way it used to be, but I know that's not a possibility right now."

Suddenly the tears came. And in that moment, the fruit gave way to the root, which allowed Nicole to finally begin to deal with the situation and her feelings about it.

There are no easy answers for how to deal with the many complexities that come from parents who separate and divorce. What I do know is that truth and honesty with how you're feeling is essential. So is professional counseling. But so, too, is the truth in God's Word, where He promises that He will never leave us or forget us (Deut. 31:8: "The LORD . . . will be with you; he will not leave you or forget you. Don't be afraid and don't worry). In fact, He promises to be even closer to the brokenhearted and to save the ones whose spirits have been crushed (Ps. 34:18:

"The LORD is close to the brokenhearted, and he saves those whose spirits have been crushed)! You can turn to God because He will never not be *with* you and will always be *for* you (Ps. 56:9: "On the day I call for help, my enemies will be defeated. I know that God is on my side).

A NEW DAY

Though we may not be able to predict every storm that comes our way or change what these storms may bring, what we do have control over is our reaction to them. The most normal natural response is fear, closely followed by doubt. Fear that you're going to get hurt. Doubt that God even cares. But the opposite is true! The Bible is filled with stories and verses that tell us our response should be to trust Him, that He's got this. In fact, one story is about an actual storm the disciples encountered while in a boat on the Sea of Galilee (Matt. 8:23–27). The crazy thing about this story is that Jesus was physically *in* the boat with them; but He was sleeping. They went to Him and said, "Lord, save us! We will drown!"

What did Jesus do? He asked them why they were afraid and where their faith was. (Think about it. Not only did they have Jesus in their lives, but He was also actually in the boat with them!) Jesus commanded the wind and the waves to stop, and instantly everything was calm. Everything was fine!

The thing about storms is that they come but they also go. They don't last forever. There's always a new day on the horizon. In the same way, not only can you know God will be with you in the storms, but He will be there afterward to help you with the changes that come. When you're turning the chairs back upright and picking up the limbs scattered across the yard, He is there. He is with you. He sees and knows and He cares.

Today, whatever you're going through, you can know that Jesus is *in* the boat with you. But you can bet He is *not* sleeping. He is simply waiting for you to call out and ask for His help.

WHAT ABOUT YOU?

In this chapter I've shared some stories that teens like you have lived and are still living—a close family member passes away, a beloved pet dies, and the horrible circumstances that come when parents divorce. Each of them represents a storm of some sort. A storm that in every regard is intense and very damaging. But through it all, as all these students would testify, the storms that came into their lives did not destroy them. Instead, they were storms of perfection.

Maybe today you're going through a storm yourself. Maybe you can relate to all of what we have shared in this chapter or maybe you can relate to none of it. Either way, storms do come. That's a promise. How you and I respond to them, well, that, my friend, will directly determine how we live out the rest of our lives.

TRUTH FROM THE CHAPTER

Let's recap a few of the truths from this chapter to internalize and remember.

- The beauty of a storm is that it's temporary.
- Everyone needs to be heard.
- God always hears us.
- Do not ignore and run from the pain that comes from loss. Instead, ask God to allow your heart to process the pain so you can move through the stages of grief and ultimately land in a place of emotional health.
- When we allow ourselves to go deep and get to the root, then what's really going on inside of us can begin to be better understood and ultimately dealt with.
- God will be with you in the storm, but He will be there afterward as well to help you with the changes that come.

TRUTH FROM GOD'S WORD

Then you will call my name. You will come to me and pray
to me, and I will listen to you. You will search for me.
And when you search for me with all your heart,
you will find me!
(Jer. 29:12–13)

God is our protection and our strength. He always helps
in times of trouble. So we will not be afraid even if the
earth shakes, or the mountains fall into the sea, even if
the oceans roar and foam, or the mountains
shake at the raging sea.
(Ps. 46:1–3)

MY PRAYER FOR YOU

Father, today I pray especially for someone who has
experienced loss. Maybe their family is going through
the separation and divorce process or it's already been
finalized, and they are now living with the results. Maybe
a family member they have been very close to has died.
Whatever the circumstance, please be close to those who
are hurting. Do what only You can do—be the Peacemaker
and the Peace-giver. Bring comfort and help them find the
joy to lift their spirits as they look to You for help and hope.
Thank You for Your promise to heal the brokenhearted. In
Jesus' name. Amen.

In the space that follows, or in a separate journal, write the answers to these questions. Since this is your story be honest with yourself. It's the only way to truly change your life forever!

Are you going through a storm right now? If so, describe it.

_____

_____

_____

_____

Do you feel heard by anyone? If so, by whom? Who hears you best?

_____

_____

_____

_____

Do you believe that Jesus cares and is with you? Whether yes or no, describe your experience and how you might be able to see it differently.

_____

_____

_____

_____

Part 2

The Path to Hope and Healing

CHAPTER 10

Is God Real?

A survey published in the *Washington Times* in 2022 stated that 54 percent of the adults in the United States believe in "God as described in the Bible."[1] The story got my attention because I would have said the percentage of believing adults was much higher than that.

I grew up in the Southeast, in what is commonly referred to as the Bible Belt. This area is known to be predominantly Christian in its belief system, and you can find an evangelical church on nearly every corner. As a child and then a teenager, I was with my family in church every time the doors were open. So instinctively I associated with the people who believed in God and didn't know many people who didn't.

Growing up in church is a good thing, and as an adult I'm now extremely grateful. It helped form a solid foundation we all need to live productive, God-honoring lives. But it can also create a false sense of security. Hearing stories from the Bible every week can cause you to believe that everything is okay with your own soul. But proximity to the truth is not enough. The truth must live inside you. It wasn't until a March afternoon, when I was twenty-one years old, that my understanding of all of this came full circle.

EVERYTHING LOOKED GREAT

From the outside looking in, it appeared as though I had the world by the tail. I was working for a real estate development company, flying from one corner of the country to another on the company's jet, and being housed at corporately owned beach condos in Florida. I was dating great-looking girls and doing whatever I wanted, whenever I wanted.

But my emotions were dangerously out of check. I was living life with a rampant arrogance. The lies I told myself and others were out of control, and I was in a bit of a tailspin.

Nothing satisfied me. Nothing filled the hollowness, the emptiness I felt deep inside. Though I was able to have and do just about whatever I wanted, it was never enough. I always came up feeling empty. I also had many fears. For instance, my mom had been very sick. In the months and years that followed, I lived with an internal awareness that she might die. I also had my own fear of mortality, constantly concerned that I might be injured. All of this daily anxiety took a serious emotional toll on me. My unwillingness to bow my heart in humble submission and make the choice to give Jesus control of my life was becoming too much for me to ignore any longer.

Early one March morning, with a lot of anger raging in my heart from the arrogance, emptiness, fear, and anxiety with which I lived life, and with absolutely no humility, I said aloud to God: "I'm in church all the time. I went to Christian schools. All my friends are Christians. But you know what? I don't believe You are real. I don't think You hear anything I'm saying. And I feel stupid right now, talking to the wind. But if by some chance I'm wrong and You really *do* exist and really *do* have a plan for my life, then *prove* it!"

Let me quickly share some valuable advice to keep in mind for the rest of your life: do not ever, under any circumstances, ask God, the Creator of the universe, to prove to you that He is real until and unless you are ready for a close encounter of the first kind. Why? Because when you invite Him to do this, He will invade your life like nothing you ever imagined!

For me, as soon as I prayed my "prove it" prayer, I was on to the next thing. I promptly left behind any hope that God would respond to my words. To be blunt, my prayer was offered with zero faith.

Sometimes, though, because He's such a good God and loves us so very much, He totally circumvents our unbelief and does something only He can do.

THE ENCOUNTER

About two and a half weeks after I prayed and asked God to prove to me that He is real, I was driving back to work after a later-than-usual lunch break. Walking into our suite of plush, well-decorated offices that beautiful afternoon, I spoke to our receptionist, Sharon, and walked to my office. I shut the door behind me, sat down, and began dialing the phone to check on a situation that needed our attention at a shopping center we had just built in West Virginia.

While dialing the phone, and with no warning whatsoever, off behind me and to the left I heard a voice clearly and calmly instruct me to "Call Mom." The words were so distinct, so audible that I twirled in my chair to see who was in my office. But I saw no one.

Not taking the time to try and figure out what was happening, I did what I had been instructed to do. I called my mom.

The phone rang six then seven times. On the eighth ring my mom answered. It was immediately apparent that something was terribly wrong. Her words were slurred, and she sounded disoriented. I suddenly knew that she was attempting suicide. She was dying, and I was hearing her life leaving her body. It was happening. The day and the moment I had been dreading, fearing for so many years was now here. My mom was dying.

In moments like these I don't think we consciously take the time to think or even to respond. Instead, we simply react, which is exactly what I did. I ran out of my office, I blew past Sharon, I jumped in my car, and I drove way over the speed limit to the little community twenty minutes to the north, where my parents lived at the time. As soon as I got in the car I called my mom again to be sure she was still alive and to also tell her to hold on, that I was on the way.

As I drove north on Interstate 75 I found that I wanted to, desperately needed to pray, to talk with this God whom I clearly did not know. I knew all about the power of prayer, but I had never experienced it and did not yet realize how much He loved and cared for me.

For the first time in many years I tried something new for me—I tried being honest. With no pretense, no big story, no fantasy world, no lies, and also with almost no faith, I simply reached out and asked God to please help my mom. Despite all that we had been through and the fragility of our relationship, as her son, I absolutely did not want my mom to die. Deep down I still yearned to be her boy and desperately needed her to love and *accept* me.

As quickly as I began to pray, God responded. In fact, as I prayed, I found myself remembering Bible verses I'd learned as a kid growing up at Ridgedale Baptist Church in Chattanooga.

Thinking back, one Sunday morning a lady named Dillie Jenkins had said to me that she saw something in me and believed that one day God was going to use me to reach a lot of people for Him. Mrs. Jenkins also believed she was supposed to help encourage me to learn Bible verses. So for every verse I memorized, she gave me ten dollars. (I memorized a lot of verses, because even as a kid I loved what money could buy.) Now, all these years later, while driving at breakneck speed to reach my mom in time, the seed of God's Word that Mrs. Jenkins had sown into my heart was producing a crop ready to be harvested.

As I raced into my parents' neighborhood and pulled into their driveway, everything looked fine. From the outside the house was probably much like the one you live in today. From the inside, however, the situation was much different. Inside, my mom was dying.

I slammed my car to a stop, jumped out, and ran to the front door. It was locked, and because I had not been given a key, my only option was to knock out a window and climb inside. Before doing that, however, I knocked and knocked and knocked. After waiting for what seemed like an eternity, my mom came down a flight of stairs, unlocked the door, and fell into my arms. I picked her up, carried her to my car, and drove her back down Interstate 75 to Parkridge Medical Center in Chattanooga.

While we were careening to the hospital that afternoon, Mom looked at me and said, "I can't be dying."

My response was immediate, "You're not going to die, Mom. But you are going to have to *choose* to live."

Choose is by far the most important word in that sentence because the choices you and I make today create the circumstances we then live with tomorrow.

Upon arriving at the hospital, we were met at the front door by nurses and an emergency room doctor. I vividly remember being shoved against a wall so Mom could be rushed into an examining room.

By this time my dad, my family, and some friends were gathered at the hospital. We waited together for forty-five minutes, with no word from anyone inside the ER. During that time I felt so alone. Sure, I knew everyone who was there, and they knew me, but because years earlier I had made the decision to not allow anyone into my heart, no intimacy in my life whatsoever, I lived a very public life in a very lonely way. If you've ever felt disconnected and all alone, even though you were surrounded by lots of people who know your name, then you know exactly how I felt.

After a while the doctor I saw when we arrived walked directly to my dad and delivered a message I will never forget.

He said, "Mr. Sikes, I have no medical reason whatsoever to share with you what I'm about to share. All I can tell you is that this is a miracle of God! Your wife is alive, she's fine, and you can go see her."

After delivering the news, the doctor, somewhat bewildered himself, turned and walked away. Dad looked at me and asked if I wanted to see my mom. I wasn't quite ready to walk into her room, so, instead, I let him know I'd be back in a few minutes. I just needed some air and to take a walk.

Miracle of God?! Are you kidding me?!

Those two thoughts chased each other round-and-round inside my mind. A medical doctor—a man who had four years of college, four years of med school, at least two years of residency, and many more years of practice—just told my dad that medicine had not saved my mom's life. *God did!*

I suddenly felt drained. Several hours had come and gone since I had dashed out of my office after a late lunch. It had been quite an emotional roller coaster. Now, all alone, leaning against a wall inside the hospital, I had an encounter with Jesus. Not a religious conversation, not a discussion about some denominational doctrine. I came face-to-face with the person of Jesus Christ Himself, the Son of the living God. His presence was undeniable! Standing there, overwhelmed by the moment, I remember saying, "You're real. You really *do* exist."

As soon as those words left my lips, I felt a sudden warm and refreshing oil-like substance on top of my head. Slowly it flowed down and into my body. With tears welling up in my eyes, I became very aware that all of the anger, pain, disappointment, and feeling that I wasn't enough, a belief I had lived with since I was four years old, were all colliding in real time with the blessing, the approval of the God of love Himself. I imagine it's hard for you to believe, but I promise you Jesus was in that hallway with me.

I had become a Christian, asking Jesus into my heart and life, at seven years of age. I knew then my heart had changed, because even at that young age I genuinely felt Him in my life. But as time went on, bringing with it the pressures of the world, I allowed my faith to become more religion in name only rather than a living, growing relationship.

In the total quietness and holiness of that moment in the hospital hallway that day, my faith was awakened, and Jesus once again became as tangible to me as He did when I was seven. Deep in my pain-ravaged heart, I not only knew that God was real but that it had been His Spirit who had instructed me to call my mom that afternoon. He was the reason she was alive.

IT WAS REAL!

Maybe what you have just read seems too good to be true or perhaps you're rolling your eyes. Either way, what I just shared with you really happened and it happened to me.

God always meets us where we are. He does it in ways so unique that only He could do them. Maybe you have not yet heard His audible voice as I did when I was twenty-one years old. Maybe you have a relationship with God that I could only hope for. Or maybe you're not sure.

All through time, people have wondered if God was real or if the stories about Him were fairy tales made to put some sort of order to the chaos of life. The Bible addresses this question in several places. Here are a few examples.

- "The heavens declare the glory of God, and the skies announce what his hands have made. Day after day they tell the story; night after night they tell it again. They have no speech or words; they have no voice to be heard. But their message goes out through all the world; their words go everywhere on earth." (Ps. 19:1–4)

- "God's anger is shown from heaven against all the evil and wrong things people do. By their own evil lives they hid the truth. God shows his anger because some knowledge of him has been made clear to them. Yes, God has shown himself to them. There are things about him that people cannot see—his eternal power and all the things that make him God. But since the beginning of the world those things have been easy to understand by what God has made. So people have no excuse for the bad things they do." (Rom. 1:18–20)
- "You believe there is one God. Good! But the demons believe that, too, and they tremble with fear." (James 2:19)

Again, I thought I had everything to make a great life, but it was never enough. I felt empty. Honestly, any time I was alone, and things got quiet, I was depressed. It wasn't until later that I learned the dissatisfaction I was feeling was because there is a space inside each of us that is reserved for God Himself. He created us with what has been described as a God-shaped hole that can only be filled with Him, His presence, His Spirit.

This is true of every human on the planet. None of us will ever be fully complete and joyfully, peacefully settled in our hearts until we have entered a personal relationship with Jesus. Not just acknowledging who He is with our minds, but giving ourselves—heart, mind, and soul—to Him, declaring He is in charge of our lives.

If you want this for you own life, then I urge you, no, I beg you to turn to page 161 in the back of this book and read "How to Know for Sure." It's the simple ABC's of how to give your heart and life to God.

Do it. I'll wait.

SUICIDE IS NEVER THE ANSWER

Suicide has become the number-one issue I encounter every day as I travel and speak. Whether in public schools, private schools, prep schools, Christian schools, alternative schools—literally everywhere we go, we come face-to-face with this killer and the results it wreaks on the lives of those left behind. Remember, hurting people hurt people. And sometimes the people the hurting people hurt most are themselves.

I have tremendous empathy for anyone who wrongly believes the lie of suicide. I am also very forthright in speaking the truth that suicide is *never* the answer.

Why?

Because God created you! He didn't need your help to birth you into this world, and He doesn't need your help to get you out of it.

Suicide is a choice that can never be undone. If you have any thoughts about ending your life, please turn to page 175 in the back of this book and find the help you so desperately want and need.

CHAPTER 11

Forgive to Find Freedom

Having been on the road and speaking in high schools for more than three decades now, I've heard a lot of stories that have caused me to pause and wonder how life could continue for the person sharing their story with me. One such story came from a young man we'll call Christopher.

After sharing stories with the students based on the message that no matter what, if you're breathing, there is still hope, I talked at length about the power of forgiveness and why it is such a significant act of faith to incorporate into our daily lives. The heart of the message is that we are freed when we forgive.

At the end of one of our presentations, Christopher asked if we could talk further about forgiveness and the power that comes from it. What he shared with me stopped me in my tracks. I had no words. After regaining a semblance of composure, I asked him to repeat what he had said to me. This time his words sank in a little deeper.

"When I was a child, I saw my dad murdered. Two years later I watched as my mom married the man who murdered my dad."

We both had tears in our eyes as we shared a moment of intense pain that will forever be time-stamped on my heart.

After we talked a little longer, we began to feel a sense of peace. I'm sure you're wondering how that could possibly happen, but it's something incredibly powerful that God gives us to guard our hearts and our minds. We feel His presence. The Spirit of God was right there, with us, as Christopher and I talked about a time in his life that followed the tragedy of both the death of his father and the remarriage of his mother, the results of which led him on a journey of pain-seeking pleasure. This journey played out in alcohol and drug addiction, which cemented the fact that hurting people hurt people, including themselves.

WHY FORGIVE?

Several times throughout this book we've mentioned the value and importance of forgiving the people who have hurt us.

- Quarterback Grant needed to forgive himself and those around him whom he felt had pressured him to perform.
- Sean was locked in his bedroom by his parents and

then institutionalized, and he needed to forgive all of them for the extreme loneliness he suffered.

- Julie needed to forgive herself for her eating disorder.
- Chip needed to forgive his abuser.
- Missy needed to forgive the school shooter, someone who had been her friend, who caused her to live the rest of her life in a wheelchair.
- Shawna had been abandoned by her first adopted father.
- Cindy had been rejected by twenty-one foster families.
- I needed to forgive the bullies who tormented me and the so-called friend who sexually abused me.

We all have someone in our lives whom we need to forgive. Forgiveness is one of those things that's a whole lot easier to talk about than to do, because talk is cheap. Forgiveness requires the hard work of intentionally deciding to release our anger and resentment toward someone who has violated us. It's a decision we make over and over again, because thoughts and memories will keep bringing everything back around.

But here's the truth we need to hold onto: Forgiveness is more for us than for the person we are forgiving. Why? Because unforgiveness is like a cancer that eats away the healthy tissue and replaces it with poisoned tissue. If left unchecked, this poison can kill us emotionally from the inside out.

Even more important is that we realize God commands us to forgive one another. Check out some verses from Matthew 6. First, the Lord's Prayer, which in verse 12 includes, "Forgive us our sins, just as we have forgiven those who sinned against us." But Jesus doesn't leave it there. Right after the "Amen" of the Lord's Prayer, He says, "Yes, if you forgive others for their sins, your Father in heaven will also forgive you for your sins. But if you don't forgive others, your Father in heaven will not forgive your sins."

Whoa! That's pretty clear!

I don't know about you, but do I want God to forgive my sins because I'm perfect? No. Are you? I'd say there's no way. It's actually impossible for humans to be perfect.

What did Jesus do before His death on the cross?

He forgave His enemies. The very people who were torturing Him and making fun of Him! Luke 23:34 reports that "Jesus said, 'Father, forgive them, because they don't know what they are doing.'" Jesus loved to the very end.

HOW DO I FORGIVE?

You've maybe heard the adage "To err is human; to forgive, divine." It's from a poem written in 1711 by the English poet Alexander Pope titled *An Essay on Criticism, Part II*. But what does it mean? In essence it's a reminder that we all make mistakes, but we should aspire to be like God in that He shows mercy and forgiveness to others. Including me. And you.

Maybe you think you haven't done anything to God. The problem with that is we all have. Just by our very existence! (Thank you, Adam and Eve.) Romans 3:23–24 tells us, "Everyone has sinned and fallen short of God's glorious standard, and all need to be made right with God by his grace, which is a free gift. They need to be made free from sin through Jesus Christ."

Hmm, okay. But it goes on for two more verses.

"God sent him to die in our place to take away our sins. We receive forgiveness through faith in the blood of Jesus' death. This showed that God always does what is right and fair, as in the past when he was patient and did not punish people for their sins. And God gave Jesus to show today that he does what is right. God did this so he could judge rightly and so he could make right any person who has faith in Jesus." (3:25–26)

Wow! There's a lot there. (You might need to read that again!)

The thing is, we have been forgiven much, and in the same way God helps us to forgive others. He poured grace, mercy, and limitless love into us to clean us up. Then He put His Holy Spirit in us to help us through the day-to-day of our lives. It's with the power of His Spirit that we can forgive others in the way God forgave us.

In a more practical sense is the how to do it. Here are a few tips from the Mayo Clinic that might help you.

- Recognize the value of forgiveness and how it can improve your life.

- Identify what needs healing and who you want to forgive.
- Join a support group or see a counselor.
- Acknowledge your emotions about the harm done to you, recognize how those emotions affect your behavior, and work to release them.
- Choose to forgive the person who's offended you.
- Release the control and power that the offending person and situation have had in your life.[1]

It takes a real commitment to make the change. It takes practice and a stick-to-itiveness, because like any other process, forgiveness can be two steps forward and sometimes one, two, or even three steps back. Which is why it also takes God's help and the power available to us through His Spirit living in us.

BUT WHAT IF I CAN'T FORGET?

The real challenge always comes with the fact that we remember things that have happened to us. Another way of saying that is that it's hard, maybe even seemingly impossible to forget something or someone who has hurt you. So what are we supposed to do when that pain comes barreling back into our brains?

I've heard it said that when those thoughts come, it helps to say, "I distinctly remember forgetting that." Say that out loud with me. "I distinctly remember forgetting that." Try it! Then take a deep breath and move on.

Here's the deal. When we *let go and let God* do His work, something powerful happens. Purposefully letting go of the control in our life, surrendering it to God, flips some kind of supernatural switch.

How about you? Does Christopher's story resemble anything in your life?

If so, I encourage you to find someone who loves God, someone you can trust, and pray about beginning a conversation like the one Christopher began with me.

Open communication permits progress. And progress brings hope.

I'm praying for you!

CHAPTER 12

The Choice of a Lifetime

We are in Louisiana, the last assembly of this week's trip, at a very large public high school and meeting the principal and hearing about the more than seventeen hundred students that will be in attendance today. Both sides of the gym will be packed. Eight hundred students on one side and nine hundred on the other, with me in the middle, talking to both sides of the large room, trusting that God will help my words connect to each heart.

Per my custom, I find a corner where I can watch the students enter and find a seat. As they walk past me, I'm praying, asking God's Holy Spirit to help me not only know what to say but when to say it.

Thirty minutes come and go very quickly. As the assembly comes to a close, I ask the three questions I always ask at the end of an event. Today, the response is staggering. Over 90 percent of the students raise their hands for one or more of the three questions. Seeing the response from both sides of the gym, I invite anyone who wants to talk about the choices they have made to join me in the center of the room. Approximately one hundred teens come forward.

While talking with one small group, a young man wearing a trench coat and rocking a very alternative look catches my eye as he rapidly moves across the gym floor and heads straight toward me. I shoot up a quick prayer, asking God for His will to be done, to include protection for all of us, and immediately peace floods my heart.

When he gets right up to me, he says, "Man, I like you. I really enjoyed your assembly. Thank you for telling me that I matter."

I smiled and said, "Man, I like you too!"

As he looked intently into my eyes, he said, "But you talked about God. I don't believe in God."

I said, "Cool. Glad I got to meet you."

At that point I turned and walked away, toward another thirty to forty students who were waiting to say hello and share some of their stories with me. That's when Zach, the boy in the trench coat, grabbed my arm and said, "I just told you I don't believe in God."

"I heard you," I replied.

"But aren't you going to try and talk me into believing in Him?" he said.

My response was immediate. "No and here's why. If I could talk you into something, someone much better than me could talk you out of it."

Zach said, "What would happen if I died right now."

I said, "Zach, are you a Christian?"

He said, "I just told you I don't believe in God."

"Well, then, you're going straight to hell," I replied.

That sentence stung the air. Zach looked at me and said, "Did you just tell me to go to hell?"

"No, Zach. You're asking questions. I'm just answering. As a Christian, I believe there is a real heaven and a real hell. Heaven is not full of good people and, conversely, hell is not full of bad people. Heaven is full of people who said yes to Jesus becoming the Lord of their life. Hell is full of people who have rejected Him."

Zach quickly replied, "Well, I go to church."

"Well, my car goes to church," I said.

The conversation slowed down then as Zach quietly said, "I got hurt in church."

"Zach, were you listening throughout the whole assembly? The reason I ask is because, during it, I shared very openly about being sexually abused by a Christian who went to church with me."

It was at that moment that Zach looked at me, and with sadness in his eyes he said, "I don't want to go to hell."

With tremendous empathy and compassion I responded, "Buddy, I don't *want* you to go to hell either. So let me ask you. Wouldn't you hate to miss heaven by thirty seconds— the time it takes to ask Jesus to come into your life and take control of everything?"

With tremendous courage, Zach again says, "I don't want to go to hell, Mr. Dean."

I agreed again and suggested he and I pray together, right then and there. Initially, he resisted. He knew that everyone would be watching him pray.

Realizing what was going on, I offered a small dose of insight by saying, "Zach, you're in the middle of a gymnasium with a long trench coat on, and it's probably a hundred degrees in here. You're speaking with the speaker. I think everybody's already watching."

Zach smiled and nodded. "Okay, let's pray."

I led him in a very simple prayer, inviting Jesus to become Lord of his life. As Zach said, "Amen," he opened his eyes. When I looked at him, I realized his eyes had changed right in front of me! Only seconds ago they were dark. Now they were full of light.

FROM DARKNESS TO LIGHT

Why is it important to understand the difference one might detect in seeing darkness instead of light in another person's eyes?

We referenced it in chapter 3, but again here's what the Bible says in Matthew 6:22–23: "The eye is a light for the body. If your eyes are good, your whole body will be full of light. But if your eyes are evil, your whole body will be full of darkness. And if the only light you have is really darkness, then you have the worst darkness."

In essence this is saying that your eyes reflect your soul. What is the soul? Your soul represents your will, your mind, your emotions. So when I saw that Zach's eyes changed and they were full of light, I recognized a significant transformation had occurred in him. From the inside out.

I asked one of our team to spend some time with Zach, talking with him about the decision he had just made and some of what's next, like finding a Bible to read and where to begin reading. (The four gospels—Matthew, Mark, Luke, and John—are a great place to begin to understand the story of Jesus.) And we coached him to find a group of people at a church to meet with on a regular basis.

When Zach and my teammate walked off together, I turned my attention back to the students who have been patiently waiting to share some of their stories with me. Ten minutes later I noticed Zach was coming back across the gym floor, but this time he had someone with him. Interrupting my conversation with another student, Zach grabbed my arm. I turned to him and said, "Hey, man, I'm talking to someone here."

Unmoved, Zach immediately responded, "Mr. Dean, this is John. John is my best friend. John is going straight to hell."

Somewhat shocked I looked at John, who asked, "What happened to my best friend?"

"That's easy," I said. "I introduced him to my best friend."

"I want what Zach has," John replied.

"It's not a what," I said. "It's a Who."

"Well, then, who is He?" John asked.

"I introduced Zach to Jesus, and Jesus is changing Zach's life!" I said.

John wanted in! He asked my help to pray with him, to ask Jesus to come to live in his heart too. So with Zack standing by his side, I led John in the same simple prayer. When John opened his eyes, the transformation was obvious in him as well—the one that occurs when Jesus takes up residence in our hearts.

As Zach and John walked off together, I heard the quiet but unmistakable voice of God inside of me say, "From the foundation of time I called Zach to be an evangelist, to tell others about Me."

Tears began to fill my eyes as I realized once again just how specific God is and how much He loves each one of us. Think about it. The very first thing Zach wanted to do after he became a Christian, after he made the choice of a lifetime, was to find his best friend and tell him about it. Zach did not want John to go one more hour without at least letting him know that God had come into his heart and radically changed his life.

A report published on June 15, 2022, by *Religion in Public* reveals the results of a survey of Gen Zers, young people ranging in age from eighteen to twenty-five (almost all surveys only contact adults), and tells us 17 percent describe their religious affiliation as either atheist or agnostic, and 31 percent say they are attached to no religion in particular. That's a total of 48 percent who are categorized as nones. In the same report, 36 percent of Gen Zers are

Christians. Only 36 percent. There is a lot of darkness out there.[1]

IT'S YOUR CHOICE TOO

How about you? What if today were the last day of your life? What if you knew you only had six hours left before this thing called life came to an end? Who would you spend those six hours with? What choices would you make? Who would you forgive? Who would you ask to forgive you? Would your attention turn toward eternity?

I believe that inside every human ever born is a space wholly reserved for a relationship with God through His Son, Jesus Christ. By the way, a relationship with Jesus is just that, a relationship, not a religion. Religion is our way to try and get to God. A relationship with Jesus in your heart is God's way to get to us.

Maybe today is your day to make the choice of a lifetime!

You might be thinking, *Dean, you've now mentioned this 'choice' thing several times in this book, even referencing a 'How to Know for Sure' page in the back. What's the big deal?*

Because your life literally depends on it.

We were created with a physical body, a soul that encompasses our mind, will, and emotions, and a spirit that allows us to connect with God. When our body dies physically what happens to us? The Bible tells us there are two destinations—heaven and hell—and the choice is up to us.

Like I said to Zach, don't be one of the many people on this planet who are going to miss being in heaven with Jesus for eternity by thirty seconds—the time it takes to pray. Instead, do what he and his friend John did and the more than three hundred thousand other kids who have signed cards at our assemblies, saying they've made the decision to follow Jesus.

It really is the choice of a lifetime.

NOW GO TELL SOMEONE

When you hear a new song you like, find a great restaurant or coffee shop, or discover the best new game to download, what do you do? You tell someone else, right? It's what friends do for each other. They share the good stuff.

The choice of a lifetime is about the good news of Jesus and what He's done for us. So why wouldn't we share that as well? Probably because it's so personal. It's not something outside of us; it's about the inside of us.

Oftentimes we only let people in so far, into those places in our lives where we feel safe enough to grant access. Most of the teenagers with whom I have spoken over the past three decades have shared with me that they really don't let people get close basically for one reason: fear. Fear of exposure, fear of betrayal, fear of rejection.

Fear is a major tool of the Enemy, but according to the Bible, fear can be eliminated from our lives. Let's see what 1 John 4:18 says about that: "Where God's love is, there is no fear, because God's perfect love drives out fear. It is punishment that makes a person fear, so love is not made perfect in the person who fears."

Perfect love—love that is mature and fully developed—is what rids us of fear.

How can you get your love to be perfected, mature, fully developed? The answer can be found in three little words tucked away in 1 John 4:16: "God is love."

When God lives in your heart, love lives in your heart.

And when love lives in you in abundance, it causes fear to be cast out of your heart.

Today, if you are wrestling with the feelings of not being able to share your faith, I'm going to suggest to you that those feelings are not true but instead are rooted in a deep fear that the Enemy has sown in your heart.

Why would he do this? Because he doesn't want the power of God, the real God, to be known. In Jesus you are a new person, no longer someone he can control. So, yeah, he can maybe scare you, but it's all smoke and mirrors. Check out 2 Corinthians 5:17, which tells us, "If anyone belongs to Christ, there is a new creation. The old things have gone; everything is made new!"

You are not alone! Your life is a life worth living because you've made the decision to live your life according to God's way. And because of that you can't help but tell others about Him! Now, even on hard days, everything truly is fine, because you have found the hope that will heal whatever comes when life hurts.

You Matter

When you look in the mirror, do you like who's staring back at you? For that matter, do you even recognize who's staring back at you? Is it the real, authentic version of yourself?

Do you think God makes mistakes? Do you believe that if you were not here, we would all be missing someone very special? Do you understand that no matter what you go through and no matter what might happen to you or because of you, there is still hope?

You matter are two words that, when embraced and received as truth, can cause even the hardest day to have significance. They are two words that will always supersede your soul's enemy's attempt to deceive you. These two words, when applied to your life, will suddenly help your life make sense. In fact, no matter where you live on Planet Earth, and despite your present circumstances, good or bad, these two words put you on an equal footing with everyone else. Romans 2:11 (NIV) explains why: "For God does not show favoritism." ʲ

What does that mean?

God loves you as much as He loves me, and He loves me as much as He loves you. There are absolutely no favorites with God.

Yes, *you matter!*

These two words have become the singular message and mission of our ministry. They have been used by God, the Creator of the universe, to transform lives at the heart level across America and around the world. You see, when you come to the complete realization that you matter—not because of what you do or not do, whose last name you share, what your GPA is, how great an athlete you are, how popular you may or may not be in school, how many likes or follows you might or might not have on social media—it changes everything.

Thinking back to Grant's story in chapter 1, you might remember that I shared Job 33:4 (NKJV) with him: "The Spirit of God has made me, and the breath of the Almighty gives me life."

I'm now going to ask you what I asked Grant.

Who made you?

Whose breath gives you life?

According to Job 33:4, the Spirit of God made you and me and the Almighty has given us life. When He put His breath into your lungs and mine, He did so because He needs us on the earth. We each have a part to play in His master plan called life.

There are other verses that confirm this. Let's look at two of them.

- "It is the Spirit that gives life. The flesh doesn't give life. The words I told you are spirit, and they give life." (John 6:63)
- "God raised Jesus from the dead, and if God's Spirit is living in you, he will also give life to your bodies that die. God is the One who raised Christ from the dead, and he will give life through his Spirit that lives in you." (Rom. 8:11)

Ever since He laid the foundations of the earth, God has had His mind on you. In fact, according to Ephesians 1, you were chosen before the world was made. He gave you a jump start with His breath into this thing called life. Think about how much He must genuinely love you because He intentionally created you! He gave you your life, a life that came directly from His life. That's pretty cool!

But remember, we also have an enemy who is constantly trying to keep us away from God. Again, from the very beginning of time, he has attempted to be God. But he's not God—he's a fallen angel who was kicked out of heaven because of his rebellion. Here are two verses that confirm who he is.

- "King of Babylon, morning star, you have fallen from heaven, even though you were as bright as the rising sun! In the past all the nations on earth bowed down before you, but now you have been cut down. You told yourself, 'I will go up to heaven. I will put my throne above God's stars. I will sit on the mountain of the gods, on the slopes of the sacred mountain. I will go up above the tops of the clouds. I will be like God Most High.'" (Isa. 14:12–14)

- "He [the devil] was a murderer from the beginning and was against the truth, because there is no truth in him. When he tells a lie, he shows what he is really like, because he is a liar and the father of lies." (John 8:44)

That's why we struggle and why, almost every day that I am on the road, some teens will make their way toward the stage. And when they muster enough courage, they will ask me, "Dean, you told me that my life matters. You don't know me. You don't know what I've done. You don't know what I believe or, for that matter, what I don't believe. You don't know anything at all about me. So how can you so confidently say that I matter?"

Maybe today, as you're reading this, you find yourself asking the same question. No sweat. Each time I get this question, or one like it, I remind them what I just shared with you.

You matter, not because of your performance.

You matter, not because you see yourself as a success or a failure.

You matter, not because of your GPA or because of your testing abilities.

You matter, not because you're a good person or a not-so-good person.

You matter, not because of your athletic ability or your theatrical ability or your inability in any the above.

There is one and only one reason why you matter. The reason begins and ends with God and His unfailing love for you. He chose to give you life. He loves you so very much that He created you. And because He created you on purpose, with purpose, and for a purpose, there is always hope. He also promises to be with you and help you when life gets hard.

And speaking of needing hope, Romans 5:5 tells us, "And this hope will never disappoint us, because God has poured out his love to fill our hearts. He gave us his love though the Holy Spirit, whom God has given to us." In this verse, God, through His Spirit, pours His love into our hearts.

Everything God does is motivated by His great love for us!

Love is why you matter.

MY PRAYER FOR YOU

My prayer for you is very simple and to the point. No matter what's going on in your world, the love of God is always as close as your next heartbeat. From this moment forward, and until you breathe your last breath or

Jesus returns for His people, I pray that you will never forget the two words that will forever change your life when everything's actually not fine at all. Two words that live as a bold reminder of truth, because you're breathing and because the love of God gave you that breath. *You matter!*

How to Know for Sure

I wish I knew how many teenagers since January 1, 1993, have asked me, "How can I know for sure that I am saved, that I'm a Christian?"

This is not only a legitimate question, it's the most important question of your life!

More times than not, the question is rooted in fear. Satan, our greatest adversary, is constantly looking for ways to defeat us. To trip us up. So even if you've given your heart, mind, and soul to God, if the Enemy can get you to doubt, to question your standing with God, then he'll do it, because the Enemy knows that he can really mess things up in your head.

So let's settle this once and for all.

The Bible tells us in Romans 10:9, "If you declare with your mouth, 'Jesus is Lord,' and if you believe in your heart that God raised Jesus from the dead, you will be saved."

Let's make this even simpler. It is the same process for everyone. We must

- Believe

- Confess
- Receive

We believe in our heart that God sent his Son Jesus to live on the earth, die on the cross for our sins, and be raised from the dead three days later.

We confess that we have sinned and ask God for forgiveness.

And then, by faith, we receive Jesus into our heart, inviting Him to be both our Lord and our Savior.

And everybody said, "Amen!"

Truth from God's Word

Throughout the book you've seen Bible verses used to explain a truth and provide a foundation for it. Because "God's Word is alive" (Heb. 4:12), it works on us when it gets inside of us. That's why I want to include a resource for you that will hopefully make it easier to ingest those words that will be like a lamp to your feet and a light to your path (Ps. 119:105).

When You Feel the Pressure to Perform

The Spirit of God has made me, and the breath of the Almighty gives me life. (Job 33:4 NKJV)

Then you will know the truth, and the truth will make you free. (John 8:32)

In all the work you are doing, work the best you can. Work as if you were doing it for the Lord, not for people. Remember that you will receive your reward from the Lord, which he promised to his people. You are serving the Lord Christ. (Col. 3:23–24)

When You Feel Isolated and Lonely

Be strong and brave. Don't be afraid of them and don't be frightened, because the LORD your God will go with you. He will not leave you or forget you. (Deut. 31:6)

Never will I leave you; never will I forsake you. (Heb. 13:5 NIV)

When You Don't Like What You See

Before I formed you in the womb I knew you, before you were born I set you apart; I appointed you as a prophet to the nations. (Jer. 1:5 NIV)

God is not a God of confusion but a God of peace. As is true in all the churches of God's people. (1 Cor. 14:33)

Do not be shaped by this world; instead be changed within by a new way of thinking. Then you will be able to decide what God wants for you; you will know what is good and pleasing to him and what is perfect. (Rom. 12:2)

I praise you because you made me in an amazing and wonderful way. What you have done is wonderful. I know this very well. (Ps. 139:14)

God has made us what we are. In Christ Jesus, God made us to do good works, which God planned in advance for us to live our lives doing. (Eph. 2:10)

God's word is true, and everything he does is right. (Ps. 33:4)

After I go and prepare a place for you, I will come back and take you to be with me so that you may be where I am. (John 14:3)

But God shows His great love for us in this way: Christ died for us while we were still sinners. (Rom. 5:8)

When You Have Been Hurt

You should know that your body is a temple for the Holy Spirit who is in you. You have received the Holy Spirit from God. So you do not belong to yourselves, because you were bought by God for a price. So honor God with your bodies. (1 Cor. 6:19–20)

"I say this because I know what I am planning for you," says the LORD. "I have good plans for you, not plans to hurt you. I will give you hope and a good future." (Jer. 29:11)

When You Are Afraid

Therefore put on the full armor of God, so that when the day of evil comes, you may be able to stand your ground, and after you have done everything, to stand. (Eph. 6:13 NIV)

Stand firm then, with the belt of truth buckled around your waist, with the breastplate of righteousness in place, and with your feet fitted with the readiness that comes from the gospel of peace. In addition to all this, take up the shield of faith, with which you can extinguish all the flaming arrows of the evil one. Take the helmet of salvation and the sword of the Spirit, which is the word of God. (Eph. 6:14–17 NIV)

Forgetting the past and straining toward what is ahead, I keep trying to reach the goal and get the prize for which God called me through Christ to the life above. (Phil. 3:13b–14)

Since you were raised from the dead with Christ, aim at what is in heaven, where Christ is sitting at the right hand of God. Think only about the things in heaven, not the things on earth. Your old sinful self has died, and your new life is kept with Christ in God. Christ is your life, and when he comes again, you will share in his glory. (Col. 3:1–4)

Human life is like grass; we grow like a flower in the field. After the wind blows, the flower is gone, and there is no sign of where it was. But the LORD's love for those who respect him continues forever and ever, and his goodness continues to their grandchildren and to those who keep his agreement and who remember to obey his orders. (Ps. 103:15–18)

But I say to you who are listening, love your enemies. Do good to those who hate you, bless those who curse you, pray for those who are cruel to you. (Luke 6:27–28)

That is why you need to put on God's full armor. Then on the day of evil you will be able to stand strong. And when you have finished the whole fight, you will still be standing. (Eph. 6:13)

A thief comes to steal and kill and destroy, but I came to give life—life in all its fullness. (John 10:10)

Where God's love is, there is no fear, because God's perfect love drives out fear. (1 John 4:18a)

My dear friends, don't try to get even. Leave room for God to show his anger. It is written, "I am the God who judges people. I will pay them back," says the Lord. (Rom. 12:19 NIRV)

When You Feel Worthless (or Superior)

Where there is no vision, the people perish. (Prov. 29:18a KJV)

You made my whole being; you formed me in my mother's body. I praise you because you made me in an amazing and wonderful way. What you have done is wonderful. I know this very well. You saw my bones being formed as I took shape in my mother's body. When I was put together there, you saw my body as it was formed. All the days planned for me were written in your book before I was one day old. (Ps. 139:13–16)

Don't judge others, or you will be judged. You will be judged in the same way that you judge others, and the amount you give to others will be given to you. (Matt. 7:1–2)

So if the Son makes you free, you will be truly free. (John 8:36)

Jesus Christ is the same yesterday, today, and forever. (Heb. 13:8)

When You Feel Disconnected and Directionless

Through his power all things were made—things in heaven and on earth, things seen and unseen, all powers, authorities, lords, and rulers. All things were made through Christ and for Christ. (Col. 1:16)

Trust the LORD with all your heart, and don't depend on your own understanding. Remember the LORD in all you do, and he will give you success. (Prov. 3:5–6)

When You Feel Rejected and Abandoned

But those who wait on the Lord shall renew their strength. (Isa. 40:31a NKJV)

Fear not, for I am with you. (Isa. 41:10a NKJV)

We also have joy with our troubles, because we know that these troubles produce patience. And patience produces character, and character produces hope. And this hope will never disappoint us, because God has poured out his love to fill our hearts. He gave us his love through the Holy Spirit, whom God has given to us. (Rom. 5:3–5)

He was hated and rejected by people. He had much pain and suffering. People would not even look at him. He was hated, and we didn't even notice him. (Isa. 53:3)

The LORD himself will go before you. He will be with you; he will not leave you or forget you. Don't be afraid and don't worry. (Deut. 31:8)

When You've Experienced a Loss

The LORD is close to the brokenhearted, and he saves those whose spirits have been crushed. (Ps. 34:18)

On the day I call for help, my enemies will be defeated. I know that God is on my side. (Ps. 56:9)

Jesus got into a boat, and his followers went with him. A great storm arose on the lake so that waves covered the boat, but Jesus was sleeping. His followers went to him and woke him, saying, "Lord, save us! We will drown!" Jesus answered, "Why are you afraid? You don't have enough faith." Then Jesus got up and gave a command to the wind and the waves, and it became completely calm. The men were amazed and said, "What kind of man is this? Even the wind and the waves obey him!" (Matt. 8:23–27)

Then you will call my name. You will come to me and pray to me, and I will listen to you. You will search for me. And when you search for me with all your heart, you will find me! (Jer. 29:12–13)

God is our protection and our strength. He always helps in times of trouble. So we will not be afraid even if the earth shakes, or the mountains fall into the sea, even if the oceans roar and foam, or the mountains shake at the raging sea. (Ps. 46:1–3)

When You Wonder If God Is Real

The heavens declare the glory of God, and the skies announce what his hands have made. Day after day they tell the story; night after night they tell it again. They have no speech or words; they have no voice to be heard. But their message goes out through all the world; their words go everywhere on earth. (Ps. 19:1–4)

God's anger is shown from heaven against all the evil and wrong things people do. By their own evil lives they hid the truth. God shows his anger because some knowledge of him has been made clear to them. Yes, God has shown himself to them. There are things about him that people cannot see—his eternal power and all the things that make him God. But since the beginning of the world those things have been easy to understand by what God has made. So people have no excuse for the bad things they do. (Rom. 1:18–20)

You believe there is one God. Good! But the demons believe that, too, and they tremble with fear. (James 2:19)

When You Need Forgiveness (or Need to Forgive)

Forgive us our sins, just as we have forgiven those who sinned against us. (Matt. 6:12)

Yes, if you forgive others for their sins, your Father in heaven will also forgive you for your sins. But if you don't forgive others, your Father in heaven will not forgive your sins. (Matt. 6:14–15)

Jesus said, "Father, forgive them, because they don't know what they are doing." (Luke 23:34)

Everyone has sinned and fallen short of God's glorious standard, and all need to be made right with God by his grace, which is a free gift. They need to be made free from sin through Jesus Christ. God sent him to die in our place to take away our sins. We receive forgiveness through faith in the blood of Jesus' death. This showed that God always does what is right and fair, as in the past when he was patient and did not punish people for their sins. And God gave Jesus to show today that he does what is right. God did this so he could judge rightly and so he could make right any person who has faith in Jesus. (Rom. 3:23–26)

When You Choose Light over Darkness

The eye is a light for the body. If your eyes are good, your whole body will be full of light. But if your eyes are evil, your whole body will be full of darkness. And if the only light you have is really darkness, then you have the worst darkness. (Matt. 6:22–23)

Where's God's love is, there is no fear, because God's perfect love drives out fear. It is punishment that makes a person fear, so love is not made perfect in the person who fears. (1 John 4:18)

God is love. (1 John 4:16)

If anyone belongs to Christ, there is a new creation. The old things have gone; everything is made new! (2 Cor. 5:17)

If you declare with your mouth, "Jesus is Lord," and if you believe in your heart that God raised Jesus from the dead, you will be saved. (Rom. 10:9)

When You Need to Know You Matter

For God does not show favoritism. (Rom. 2:11 NIV)

It is the Spirit that gives life. The flesh doesn't give life. The words I told you are spirit, and they give life. (John 6:63)

God raised Jesus from the dead, and if God's Spirit is living in you, he will also give life to your bodies that die. God is the One who raised Christ from the dead, and he will give life through his Spirit that lives in you. (Rom. 8:11)

Because of his love, God had already decided to make us his own children through Jesus Christ. That was what he wanted and what pleased him, and it brings praise to God because of his wonderful grace. (Eph. 1:5–6)

King of Babylon, morning star, you have fallen from heaven, even though you were as bright as the rising sun! In the past all the nations on earth bowed down before you, but now you have been cut down. You told yourself, "I will go up to heaven. I will put my throne above God's stars. I will sit on the mountain of the gods, on the slopes of the sacred mountain. I will go up above the tops of the clouds. I will be like God Most High." (Isa. 14:12–14)

He [the devil] was a murderer from the beginning and was against the truth, because there is no truth in him. When he tells a lie, he shows what he is really like, because he is a liar and the father of lies. (John 8:44)

And this hope will never disappoint us, because God has poured out his love to fill our hearts. He gave us his love though the Holy Spirit, whom God has given to us. (Rom. 5:5)

Suicide Is Never the Answer

Where there is life and breath, there is hope. Suicide is never, ever the answer.

Maybe you simply need to know there is someone available to help you. Someone who understands and is willing to take the time to share part of your life with you. If so, there is a national organization that specializes in suicide prevention. They have people available on their lifeline 24/7/365.

Both 988lifeline.org and youmatter.us share this truth: We can all help prevent suicide.

The 988 Lifeline provides free and confidential support 24/7/365 for people in distress as well as prevention and crisis resources for you and your loved ones and best practices for professionals in the United States.

Dial 988

The life you save may be your own!

Notes

Aisle 21 at Home Depot

1. Finkelhor D, Turner HA, Shattuck A, Hamby SL. "Prevalence of Childhood Exposure to Violence, Crime, and Abuse: Results from the National Survey of Children's Exposure to Violence," *JAMA Pediatrics* (2015), 169(8):746–754, doi:10.1001/jamapediatrics.2015.0676.
2. "National Statistics on Child Abuse, *National Children's Alliance*," National Children's Alliance (2024), https://www.nationalchildrensalliance.org/media-room/national-statistics-on-child-abuse.
3. "What Are the Statistics of the Abused?" *National Association of Adult Survivors of Child Abuse* (2011), http://www.naasca.org/2012-Resources/010812-StaisticsOfChildAbuse.htm.
4. "What's an Emotional Wound?" *The Journal That Talks Back*, (2023), https://www.thejournalthattalksback.com/blog/what-is-an-emotional-wound-and-how-can-we-heal-from-it.

Chapter 2

1. "Adolescent Behaviors and Experiences Survey—United States, January–June 2021," *Centers for Disease Control and Prevention*, Morbidity and Mortality Weekly Report (April 1, 2022), https://www.cdc.gov/mmwr/volumes/71/su/pdfs/su7103a1-a5-H.pdf, 16, 19–20.

Chapter 3

1. Jannik Lindner, "Body Image Teenager Statistics: Market Report & Data," Gitnux (December 20, 2023), https://gitnux.org/body-image-teenager-statistics/.
2. José Francisco López-Gil, Antonio García-Hermoso, Lee Smith, et al., "Global Proportion of Disordered Eating in Children and Adolescents: A Systematic Review and Meta-analysis," *JAMA Pediatrics* 177, no. 4 (2023): 363–372; doi:10.1001/jamapediatrics.2022.5848; https://jamanetwork.com/journals/jamapediatrics/fullarticle/2801664.

Chapter 5

1. Michela Moscufo, "Survivors of Kentucky school shooting recall deadly day, 25 years later," *ABC News* (October 14, 2022), https://abcnews.go.com/US/survivors-kentucky-school-shooting-recall-deadly-day-25/story?id=91448795.
2. WPSD Staff, "Heath 20 Years Later: Michael Carneal," *WPSD Local 6* (November 28, 2027), https://www.wpsdlocal6.com/archive/heath-20-years-later-michael-carneal/article_7322a973-541d-56a7-85ed-1f62bfefae7e.html.
3. Michela Moscufo, "Survivors of Kentucky school shooting recall deadly day," *ABC News* (October 14, 2022), https://abcnews.go.com/US/survivors-kentucky-school-shooting-recall-deadly-day-25/story?id=91448795.

4. Brad Ricca, "The first U.S. school shooting was in 1853. Its victim was a teacher," *Washington Post* (May 25, 2022), https://www.washingtonpost.com/history/2022/05/25/first-school-shooting-louisville-ward-butler/.

5. "History of School Shootings in the United States," K12 Academics (2004–2024), https://www.k12academics.com/school-shootings/history-school-shootings-united-states.

6. David Riedman, "School Shootings in the United States," K–12 School Shooting Database (2024), https://k12ssdb.org/data-visualizations (accessed May 6, 2024).

7. "Latest News, Tips, Guides about Education," 21K School (June 5, 2024), https://www.21kschool.world/ge/blog/school-shooting-statistics-2023/.

8. Christopher Wolf, "School Shootings by State: Nearly 350 school shooting incidents occurred across the U.S. in 2023, data shows," *U.S. News & World Report* (January 5, 2024), https://www.usnews.com/news/best-states/articles/states-with-the-most-school-shootings.

9. Columbia Broadcasting Network, 2022 interview with Missy Jenkins. "Forgiving Heart Escaped Paralysis," CBN (December 10, 2022), https://www2.cbn.com/article/not-selected/forgiving-heart-escaped-paralysis.

10. "2022–2023 Violence in Schools Report," *Educator's School Safety Network* (2023), https://eschoolsafety.org/violence.

11. Becton Loveless, "Bullying Epidemic: Facts, Statistics and Prevention," *Education Corner* (January 16, 2024), https://www.educationcorner.com/bullying-facts-statistics-and-prevention/. The note "National Education Association" refers to a 2012 press release that is no longer available online. The note "Petrosina, Guckenburg, Devoe and Hanson 2010" refers to Anthony Petrosino, Sarah Guckenburg, Jill DeVoe, and Thomas Hanson,

What Characteristics of Bullying, Bullying Victims, and Schools Are Associated with Increased Reporting of Bullying to School Officials? Issues & Answers Report, REL (2010): No. 092 (Washington, DC: Institute of Education Sciences, 2010).

Chapter 6

1. U. S. Department of Health and Human Services, "Effects of Bullying," *Stop Bullying.gov* (May 21, 2021), https://www.stopbullying.gov/bullying/effects.

Chapter 7

1. Jonathan Rothwell, "Teens Spend Average of 4.8 Hours on Social Media Per Day," *Gallup* (October 13, 2023), https://news.gallup.com/poll/512576/teens-spend-average-hours-social-media-per-day.aspx.
2. Tara Well, "The Hidden Danger of Online Beauty Filters: The more you edit your image, the greater the harm," *Psychology Today* (March 25, 2023), https://www.psychologytoday.com/us/blog/the-clarity/202303/can-beauty-filters-damage-your-self-esteem.

Chapter 9

1. Andy Andrews, *Storms of Perfection: In Their Own Words,* 4 vols. (Nashville: Lightning Crown, 1991).
2. See Elisabeth Kübler-Ross, *On Death and Dying* (New York: Macmillan, 1969).

Chapter 10

1. Sean Salai, "Survey: 54% of U.S. adults believe in 'God of the Bible,'" Washington Times (March 22, 2022),

https://www.washingtontimes.com/news/2022/mar/22/
survey-54-us-adults-believe-god-bible.

Chapter 11

1. Mayo Clinic Staff, "Forgiveness: Letting go of grudges and bitterness," *Mayo Clinic* (November 22, 2022), https://www.mayoclinic.org/healthy-lifestyle/adult-health/in-depth/forgiveness/art-20047692.

Chapter 12

1. Paul A. Djupe and Jacob R. Neiheisel, "How future Supreme Court rulings ruling [sic] may fuel the decline of religion in the US," Religion in Public (July 15, 2022), https://religioninpublic.blog/2022/07/15/how-future-supreme-court-rulings-ruling-may-fuel-the-decline-of-religion-in-the-us.

Thanks

Each time we begin a new project in our ministry, especially writing a new book for teens and their families, we know going into it that much time will be required in prayer, in the Word, the preparation, in the writing, in the edits—all the components that go into creating the finished resource.

For all of the above to happen, everything is on a scheduled timeline.

Time, our most precious commodity, is something I cherish the most with God and with my family. And so, for the time the Lord took with me as I wrote this book, I'm eternally grateful.

For the time away from my family to get alone and quiet so I could invest the necessary time to tune in to His frequency, so in turn I could hear and see what He wanted me to write, I'm so very thankful.

To my wife, Lori, who is my biggest cheerleader and simultaneously, the one who always tells me the truth in love, I love you, Lu, and am so very thankful for you.

To Scott Hamilton, my dear friend who one day said to me, "I need to introduce you to Debbie Wickwire." Thank you for being sensitive to the Spirit of God and thank you for the introduction.

To Debbie Wickwire, your content editing stretched me, challenged me, and brought out of me that which became the book God called us to create. You have a true gift and for you and for what you do, I am so very thankful.

To Mary Hollingsworth and your Creative Enterprises Studio team, thank you for the hours you invested into ensuring the finished manuscript matches what the Lord birthed in my heart when He led me to begin the journey of writing this book.

To our ministry partners who helped make this book a reality, you share in the rewards of all the lives who catch the revelation as they read this book that yes, THEY MATTER.

And finally, to our YOU MATTER team, thank you to each of you for the role you play in our mission, our vision, and the day-to-day operations that make what we do a reality. Lori and I would not want to be on this journey of hope without you.

About the Author

Since January 1993, Dean Sikes has crisscrossed the United States and traveled internationally to minister in public and private high schools, teen challenge centers, and prisons. To date he's spoken at more than four thousand events, sharing God's message of hope with millions of teenagers.

In addition to traveling, Dean hosts You Matter TV, a national television broadcast that is aired four times each week on multiple networks across the country.

A published author, Dean has written thirty-two books that serve as follow-up resources for teens and their families.

The connection he has with teens and young people continues to ignite a conversation that encompasses these truths: God loves you. He's got a plan for your life. And because you're breathing, you matter.

Dean, his wife, Lori, and their family make their home in Tennessee.

YOU MATTER

An Outreach of the Spirit of America Foundation

A 501(c)(3) Corporation

Post Office Box 8915

Chattanooga, Tennessee 37414

WWW.YOUMATTER.US

HOPE 365
A Devotional for Teens

Dean Sikes

In *HOPE 365: A Devotional for Teens* you have the opportunity to take a few minutes every day to hang out with God and His Word. As you do, you can experience God's presence and His promises through these special messages.

These daily devotionals deal with the kinds of challenges you may face as a teenager, and they will offer you help and hope every day.

Scan the code below now to download your free e-Book of HOPE 365!

FREE!
e-Book   **YOUMATTER.us**

Made in the USA
Coppell, TX
07 November 2024